D1622851

The Pink Magnolia

The resemblance of any character in this novel to any person, living or dead, is not intended. The characters, events, and locations are completely fictional. However, since we all have a dark side, each of us just might see ourselves in one or more of the people that reside in the fictional community of Falls City, Georgia.

WWW.EPISKOPOLS.COM
Books for Clergy and the People They Serve

Copyright © 2008 Dennis R. Maynard
All rights reserved.
ISBN: 1-4392-0016-5
ISBN-13: 978-1439200162

Visit www.booksurge.com to order additional copies.

DENNIS R. MAYNARD

THE PINK
MAGNOLIA
BOOK FOUR IN
THE MAGNOLIA SERIES

2008

The Pink Magnolia

OK! I have read books one and two; I am almost afraid to start number three as I don't want my visit with Father Steele to be over. These are awesome books.

Jackie Maronski
Augusta, Georgia

This past fall I ordered "Behind the Magnolia" and "When the Magnolia Blooms"—they were received—and read! Enjoyed them both so much. I laughed and cried, sometimes at the same time. I hope there are others in the offing.

The Reverend Netha N. Brada
Iowa Falls, Iowa

I wish you could do something about that Bishop! I want somebody other than God to straighten him out, and I want to hear about it! I felt like I was walking beside Steele every step he made. Found it hard to put down at night to sleep!

Anna McCoy
Houston, Texas

The novels arrived yesterday and they're dutifully farmed out to different people in the congregation who were eagerly awaiting them….they'll be dog-eared before the year is out and no doubt the subject of further conversation.

The Reverend Michael D. Reddig
Cambridge, Maryland

I just finished reading "Behind the Magnolia Tree." I couldn't put it down! What a great read! I really enjoyed your writing style and it seemed like every page read just made me want to keep on reading. I especially love all the strong southern names—Steele, Stone, Almeda, Chadsworth. I can't wait to get started on the next book...

John Wright
La Quinta, California

My husband and I have read your books on long drives. We have both enjoyed the series and await the next chapter where I am hoping you "prune" Rufus and get Steele elected Bishop. While reading your last book we were making up suggestions for your next one and agreed that "Chain Sawing the Magnolia" might be appropriate. I am pleased you ended on a happier note. We look forward to the next chapter and verse...

Helen Taylor
Port Isabel, Texas

I have just completed the "Magnolia Series" and enjoyed the books very much. As a nurse educator in the Sharp Healthcare System, I plan to make reference to them to assist the nursing staff with communication and forgiveness which I feel will enhance teamwork on the nursing unit.

Rosalind Duddy
Poway, California

I finished "Pruning the Magnolia Tree" over a week ago and am going through withdrawal! I see many of your characters on a daily basis. Those in my husband's Bible Study group anxiously await our finishing each book so we can pass them around. Many have purchased them as gifts for family and friends. Please keep the series alive and take us back to Falls City as quickly as possible.

Connie S. Miles
Laredo, Texas

We have thoroughly enjoyed your books and we eagerly await the next one in the series. They are quickly being circulated around our parish.

Leslie Ross
Boca Raton, Florida

I just finished "Behind the Magnolia", I loved it. I have been an Episcopalian all my life. I can relate to so much in it that it is scary. I just started the second book and am having a hard time putting it down. I hope many more stories will come out of First Church.

Elizabeth Lorenzen
Brawley, California

Just finished reading Behind the Magnolia Tree. I loved it. I believe that everyone contemplating the ordained ministry should be made to read it. You captured the intensity and commonality of what it means to be a rector. I don't know how many times I was chuckling "that's me." I thoroughly enjoyed the whole thing.

The Reverend Richard Sanders, D. Min
Augusta, Georgia

Like the two prior books in the series, "Behind the Magnolia" and "When the Magnolia Blooms," the third book is just as hard to put down. Several story lines are masterfully interwoven into a fast-paced drama that offers remarkable insight into the life of a parish priest. The characters are colorful and the stories are compelling. Great read!

Patrick Blythe
Palm Desert, California

BOOKS BY
DENNIS R. MAYNARD

THOSE EPISKOPOLS

This is a popular resource for clergy to use in their new member ministries. It seeks to answer the questions most often asked about the Episcopal Church.

FORGIVEN, HEALED AND RESTORED

This book is devoted to making a distinction between forgiving those who have injured us and making the decision to reconcile with them or restore them to their former place in our lives.

THE MONEY BOOK

The primary goal of this book is to present some practical teachings on money and Christian Stewardship. It also encourages the reader not to confuse their self-worth with their net worth.

FORGIVE AND GET YOUR LIFE BACK

This book teaches the forgiveness process to the reader. It's a popular resource for clergy and counselors to use to do forgiveness training. In this book, a clear distinction is made between forgiving, reconciling, and restoring the penitent person to their former position in our lives.

BEHIND THE MAGNOLIA TREE

When the Gospel of a young Episcopal priest conflicts with the secrets of sex, greed, and power in an old southern community, it can mean only one thing for the youthful outsider, even if he is ordained. His idealism places him in an ongoing conflict with the bigotry and prejudice that are in the historical fabric of the community.

WHEN THE MAGNOLIA BLOOMS

This is the second book in the Magnolia Series. Steele Austin finds himself in the middle of a murder investigation. Those antagonistic to his ministry continue to find new ways to attempt to rid themselves of the young idealist. And through it all, the work of the Church goes on. Miracles of work and mercy do occur.

PRUNING THE MAGNOLIA

Steele Austin's vulnerability increases even further when he uncovers a scandal that will shake First Church to its very foundation. A most unusual pastoral situation cements him in an irrevocable bond with one of his most outspoken antagonists.

THE PINK MAGNOLIA

Will Steele and Randi leave Falls City? The antagonists have a new plan. A central character dies. And then, the book ends with the most anxiety-filled cliffhanger yet.

THE SWEET MAGNOLIA

Coming in the fall of 2009.

All of Doctor Maynard's books can be viewed and ordered on his website
WWW.EPISKOPOLS.COM

BOOKS FOR CLERGY AND THE PEOPLE THEY SERVE

ACKNOWLEDGEMENTS

I continue to be grateful to all the Rectors and bookstore managers across the nation that have invited me to preach for them and do book signings. From Chicago to Houston and from Virginia to California, bookstore managers have not only stocked these books, but along with their Rectors, they have actively recommended them to their customers.

The list of clergy that are utilizing the books in the Magnolia Series for discussion in their congregations is lengthy, but I would be remiss not to acknowledge you in this writing. I am grateful to each of my brothers and sisters that wear the collar. I am grateful to each of you that use my novels in your book clubs and discussion groups.

I owe a special word of appreciation to Tom and Deborah Marchant of Greenville, South Carolina and Pawleys Island, South Carolina respectively. They, along with Jo Nell King, played both supportive and inspirational roles in the production of this particular novel. This same gratitude goes to so many of the full time and seasonal residents of the *arrogantly shabby* community known simply as *Pawleys* to those who love her.

I want to express my appreciation to Jean and Julian Hunt, also of Greenville, South Carolina. Their cat, Bogey, graciously shared his home with us at Pawleys Plantation on *the Island* so that I could write and rewrite this manuscript. Bogey guards the house with diligence. He took delight in watching me for hours each day as some unseen force allowed this story to unfold through my fingertips. Bogey became my brand new very best friend.

I want to also acknowledge The Reverend Nancy Sinclair and all the residents of Leisure World in Seal Beach, California. This same heartfelt gratitude is extended to The Reverend Ella Breckenridge and the members of St. Thaddeus Episcopal Church in Aiken, South Carolina. My appreciation and support for the "Remain Episcopal" group in the Diocese of San Joaquin must also be noted. They, along with the dedicated people at Our Saviour Parish in Hanford, California, have my admiration and loyalty.

My wife, Nancy, continues to be one of my best critics and supporters. My sons Dennis Michael, Andrew and his wife Kristin Zanavich, and our daughter, Kristen Anne, have been steadfast with their words of encouragement.

My heartfelt thanks to each of you that have read the words that I put on paper. I am also grateful to you for recommending my books to others. With each book I am reminded once again that these words come through me, but they are not from me.

Dennis Maynard, D. Min.
Rancho Mirage, California
Pentecost, 2008

This Book Is For Our Soon To Be Born Grandchild. We Don't Yet Know Your Name, But We Can Hardly Wait To See Your Face.

BOOK FOUR

The Church is a hospital for sinners. It is not a museum for saints.

CHAPTER 1

The Right Reverend Rufus Petersen was sitting in his favorite purple arm chair. He had placed it next to the window in his office overlooking the Cathedral gardens. He had returned all of his telephone calls before lunch. He had no appointments for the day so he was able to catch up on his correspondence. He was particularly pleased with the letter that he'd written to the Rector of First Church in Falls City. He was so proud of it that he'd had his secretary both fax a copy to him in Falls City and send him a hard copy through the mail. Finally, he felt like he'd put that sorry excuse for a priest in his place. For lunch he'd walked across the street to a little bistro. As he settled in his chair to read one of his favorite mystery novelists, he felt like the Reuben sandwich he had eaten was still lodged in his throat.

He pushed the intercom button on the telephone sitting on the table next to his chair. His secretary answered, "Yes, Bishop. What can I do for you?"

"Do we have anything carbonated out there? I need something to help me digest that damn sandwich."

"I'll look in the refrigerator, Bishop. I think I saw a Coca-Cola earlier. I'll bring it to you."

Rufus sat back and picked up the novel. He tried to belch, thinking that would bring him some relief, but he couldn't get anything to come up. He started reading. He was excited about this particular book. He had scanned the pages when he purchased it at the neighborhood bookstore. The murders were described in a particularly gruesome detail. Bishop Rufus Petersen anticipated reading the descriptions over and over again. He tried another belch. He found no relief. Instead, he felt a sharp pain in his left jaw that shot up the side of his face. It radiated down his neck into his left arm. He broke out in a cold sweat. He was having difficulty breathing. He tried to stand but fell forward onto the floor. His neck and arm were now numb. He felt as though he was going to vomit.

Then the Bishop of Savannah heard a ringing in his ears. It was deafening. He felt himself being drawn through a tunnel. There were swirling multi-colored lights all around him. He was flying at lightning speed toward a bright light at the end of a tunnel. He exited the tunnel and realized that he was outside his own body. The ringing had stopped. There were no bright lights. He was floating over his own body. His body was lying on the floor of his office. He could see his secretary pushing on his chest and blowing into his mouth. Her face was covered with tears.

"Rufus...Rufus," he heard a familiar voice calling to him. He looked to his left and saw his sainted mother. She was absolutely radiant. She was more beautiful than he remembered her. She was extending her hand toward him. She was smiling. "Rufus, take my hand. I've been waiting on you."

"Momma, is that really you?" Then Rufus realized that he was talking to his mother and she was talking to him, but their lips weren't moving. They were literally reading one another's hearts. "Momma, what is this place? Where am I? It's absolutely beautiful here." He stretched out his hand towards his mother's outstretched hand. He tried to move toward her. He wanted to hug her. But some force kept him from approaching her. It was as though there was an invisible wall separating them. "Momma, help me. I can't move!"

She shook her head. "I'm sorry, son. That just means it's not yet your time. You're going to have to go back."

"No!" Rufus heard his own heart scream. "I don't want to go back. I want to stay here with you. I want to be with you."

"It's no use." She reassured him. "I'll be waiting here for you. Next time you'll get to stay here with me."

"No, Momma," Rufus pleaded. "Don't make me go back."

"It's not up to me, my darling boy. I can't keep you here. You still have work to do back there."

Rufus felt a pain in his chest. "Stop that!" he shouted. It was as though his entire chest was on fire. The painful burn was incredible. "Help me, Momma, my chest hurts."

She smiled at him again. "Rufus, before you go back I have to tell you that I'm very disappointed in you. You need to go back and make some changes in your life. You need to be a different kind of person. You can do better."

Rufus complained. "What are you talking about? I'm doing the best I know how to do."

"No Rufus, you're not. You know how to be different. You need to do as I have told you. Please, don't disappoint me." And then she began to fade away. In an instant she was gone.

"Ouch!" Once again Rufus felt a sharp pain in his chest. His entire body was on fire. Everything around him began to whirl. There were multi-colored lights everywhere. He was being drawn through them at lightning speed. Everything around him was spinning. Then, in an instant, he realized he was back in his body. He heard someone say, "I have a pulse." He heard another voice shout, "We have sinus rhythm! Let's transport him."

His entire body was in pain. He was struggling to breathe. He could hear his secretary crying, "Oh, thank you, Jesus. Thank you, Jesus." He wished she would just shut up. "Rufus, you're going to be all right. These ambulance people are going to get you to the hospital. You're going to be just fine, Bishop. You're going to be just fine. Hang in there."

He felt himself being lifted onto a bed. No, he heard the snap of a metal frame. He realized it was a stretcher. He was moving. He was outside. He felt the warmth of the sun on his face. A gentle breeze brushed across him. Then he felt himself being lifted up. He struggled to open his eyes and realized he was being lifted into an ambulance. Someone shouted, "Move! We need to get him there quick!" Then he heard the whirl of a siren. Something was in his nose. It was itching. He tried to reach up and remove it but a strong hand stopped him. "That's your oxygen," he heard the stranger's voice say. Once again he opened his eyes so he could see who was talking to him. Then he felt another sharp pain in his heart. He grabbed his chest. He couldn't breathe. He relaxed into the stretcher, struggling for breath. Then everything went dark. There was nothing but blackness all around him.

CHAPTER 2

Randi and Steele Austin had talked beyond midnight. They both awoke early and talked some more. They had made a decision. A bit of anxiety remained in both of them. They were not one hundred percent sure they had made the right decision. At least they did not have to live with the indecision. St. Jude's in San Antonio was a tremendous opportunity. They told each other that opportunities like that just don't come around every day. Ultimately their decision had to be based on the type of ministry Steele wanted to exercise. If they stayed at First Church his ministry would be defined in one way. If they moved to San Antonio it would be defined in a diametrically opposite way. It was not just a decision about accepting or declining a call. It was a decision about the type of ministry he wanted to have.

Steele did not go through his secretary's office when he stepped off the elevator in the First Church Parish House. He used the key to his private entrance. He knew he had to make a telephone call and he needed to make it first thing. He must not become distracted by anything. He walked directly to his desk. He didn't even turn on his office lights. He picked up the telephone and dialed the number in San Antonio, Texas that had become so familiar to him. He had a direct line into the office of Charles Gerard. "Father Austin, when can I order up the moving van? I tell you our entire parish is so excited about you folks coming to St. Jude's. We tried to keep it a secret that we'd issued you the call, but the Vestry just couldn't do it. What moving company do you want to use?"

A sick feeling came over Steele. "Charles, this is one of the most difficult telephone calls I've ever had to make."

"Oh no, I don't like the sound of that. I sure hope this isn't going the direction I think it's headed."

"I'm so sorry, Charles. Randi and I fell in love with you. We fell in love with all the people that we met. We loved San Antonio. It excites us to think about the possibility of moving closer to our families. And Charles, I really think we're a good match for St. Jude's."

"Then what's the problem, Father? Do you want more money? We've just offered you a starting package. There's more to follow. Tell me what you want and I'll get it done."

"Charles, it's not about money. You folks have made an offer that far exceeds our expectations. You are very generous."

"Then what is it?"

"I guess the bottom line is that I feel needed here."

Charles Girard raised his voice. "Needed? Father Austin, I've done my homework on that place. We treat bulls we're about to castrate more humanely than that parish has treated you and your family. And that Bishop of yours is actively working to undermine your ministry. Now, just why do you think those people need you?"

"I understand exactly what you're saying. Randi and I also know that you're absolutely right. St. Jude's is a wonderful place. It's in a growing suburb. You folks have everything going for you. You can't help but be a success. Honestly, Charles, your parish is the dream call for an awful lot of clergy. I think your next Rector's biggest challenge will be to get out of the way and just let your parish continue to grow and prosper. You're going to be a major parish. Maybe you'll even be the biggest parish in Texas before it's all over."

"Didn't you get excited about building a new church? You realize that's our next major project. We're full every Sunday at every service already. We've got to build a bigger and more magnificent sanctuary. Don't you want to be a part of that?'

"Charles, I know all that could be very exciting. What priest couldn't get excited about it?"

"Well, evidently you can't."

"No, please don't take me wrong. It just boils down to need. I really feel like these people here need me. They've just gone through a very difficult time. One of their most trusted staff members betrayed them. I think it's a very critical time in the life of this congregation. And beyond that, some of these folks need me individually as their pastor. A couple of my parish leaders are going through some really ugly stuff in their lives. I just don't feel like I can walk away from them. I feel like if I left them right now I would leave them as sheep without a shepherd. I just can't bring myself to do it."

"And that's the very quality in you that makes you a good priest, Father Austin. That's one of the things we saw in you. That's only one of the reasons we wanted you to be our Rector."

"Thanks for understanding, Charles."

There was a long silence on the line. Then Charles spoke, "I can't tell you how disappointed I am personally and just how disappointed our people are going to be."

"I know. I really wish that the timing was different. I just wish that I had two lives so that I could give the good folks at St. Jude's one of them. But Charles, I really do believe that your success as a parish is inevitable. Just don't call someone who'll mess things up for you. In all honesty, I really don't think they have to be all that talented. Your parish is on the move and the only way that you will be able to stop growing is to just stop trying. But these people need me right now and I simply can't walk away from them. That really is the bottom line. It's just that simple."

"I understand. Let's stay in touch, Father Austin. I feel like I've found a friend in you. I'm going to watch your ministry with great interest. I'd like to call you from time to time to talk with you if that's acceptable."

"Charles, I'd like nothing better. And I'll watch St. Jude's with an equal amount of interest. I hope you'll get your new Rector to invite me to come and preach from the pulpit in your wonderful new church when it's finished."

"You just consider that a done deal. God bless you and your family, Father."

"And God bless you and St. Jude's, Charles."

With that both men hung up their respective telephones. Steele immediately picked up his receiver again to make one more call. "Did you call him?" Randi asked.

"It's done. He was understanding, but really disappointed."

"How do you feel?"

"I'm still a little uneasy...even a bit sick to my stomach."

"Do you still think we made the right decision?"

"Only time will tell, but right now I'm even less sure than before I made the call. I'm not at complete peace with it."

"Me either."

"Do you want me to call him back and tell him I've changed my mind?"

"No, Steele. I know you. I know the kind of ministry you want. You would be a big hit at St. Jude's. I have no doubt about that. You could have a successful ministry there. But Steele, Honey, it's not the kind of ministry that brings you the greatest joy. I think for now, those opportunities are right here at First Church."

"Thanks for that. I know you're right. My head tells me you're right. My heart just isn't completely convinced."

"I know. Have I told you today that I love you?"

"And have I thanked you today for loving me?"

"Yes, you do it all the time. I've got to go. Call me later?"

"I'll look forward to it."

CHAPTER 3

Henry Mudd was in Las Vegas to see a new client that had bought a carpet factory near Falls City. He booked himself into the Wynn Hotel. His business with his client had only taken three hours. He had the rest of the day free. He walked the strip. He went in and out of the various hotels and casinos. He was surrounded by people, but he had never felt more alone in his entire life. He stopped in Caesar's Palace and made his way to a poker machine. He put a hundred dollar bill in the machine. He began playing. In a matter of just a few plays he was down twenty dollars. A young woman in a very tight uniform that exposed the tops of her ample bosom approached him. She was carrying a drink tray. "Would you like a complimentary drink?"

Henry nodded. "Yes, thank you ma'am. Bourbon on the rocks would be nice." He continued to play. By the time she returned he had regained his lost twenty and was up forty more. She bent over to serve him his drink. When she did the tops of her breasts poured out over the top of her uniform. Henry stared. He began to feel a stirring that he had not had in months. He quickly emptied his glass. He smiled at the young woman. He reached in his pocket and took a twenty dollar bill from his money clip. He put it on the tray along with his empty glass. "Keep them coming."

She smiled a knowing smile.

Henry finally called it quits after he had lost five hundred dollars to the machine. He had been up several times, but then the cards turned against him. He walked away a loser. In fact, he was an inebriated loser. He strolled out of Caesar's Palace. The water show was a real crowd pleaser. He stood with the rest of the tourists and watched the fountains dance to light and music. When it was over he walked down the walkway and back onto the strip. The desert night air felt good. He knew he had too much to drink, but he simply didn't care. He decided to walk the few blocks back to the Wynn. Along the route there were men handing out flyers of some sort. He took one of them. It was an advertisement for female dancers. There were pictures of beautiful young women. The advertisement included a telephone number. You only needed to call the number and one of these beauties would come to your hotel room and dance in private for you. Henry put the flyer in his pocket.

Back at his room he stretched out on the bed. He knew he would not be able to relax. Whenever he tried to turn off his mind his thoughts inevitably returned to the videos of his wife with another man. He began to think he would never get over the sick feeling those images brought him. He had turned the actual videos over to a divorce attorney. They were no longer in his physical possession. The problem was that he couldn't get them out of his head. Often he would wake up in the middle of the night in a cold sweat. Memories of those same videos would shake his dream world. He had moved to the guest bedroom suite. He found it difficult even to look at his wife. The thought of touching her repulsed him. He had hoped that moving out of their shared bedroom would bring him some relief. None had come. He reached into his pocket and brought out the leaflet he had been handed. He shouted, "At least these girls have enough sense to charge for it, Virginia. Hell, you were out there giving it away."

He got up and went to the mini-bar in his room. He continued to shout to some unseen presence, "Virginia, the damn whores on this leaflet are a better class of slut than you are!"

Their daughters had asked why they didn't sleep in the same room anymore. Henry explained to them that their mother had started snoring so loudly it was interrupting his rest. "Why am I the one that has to be snoring so loud?" Virginia complained. "Why can't you be the problem?" Henry just glared at her. She started crying, but he didn't care.

He poured himself another glass of bourbon. The leaflet was on the bed. He picked it up. He stared at the pictures of the girls. His mind flashed back to the cocktail waitress. He thought about her breasts. He thought about her smile. Once again he felt himself stir. He picked up the telephone and dialed the number on the leaflet. "LV Dancers, how can we help you?"

"I would like for you to send a girl to room 1508 in the Tower Suites at the Wynn Hotel."

"Yes, sir, do you have any preferences?"

Henry studied the faces on the leaflet. There was a young woman that looked a lot like the cocktail waitress. "Yes, I have one of your leaflets here. Send me Gigi."

"Excellent choice," the voice on the other end of the telephone responded. "She is one of our best dancers. Now how would you like to pay?"

"Do you take credit cards?"

"Yes, we take all the major credit cards. The fee is 250.00 dollars for one hour. The charge will appear on your bill as Brown Distribution Center. Is that agreeable?"

"Sure." Henry gave the voice his credit card number.

"Sir, you understand that you have paid for Gigi to come to your room to dance for you for one hour?"

"Yes."

"If you make any other arrangements with Gigi those arrangements are by mutual consent and strictly between the two of you."

"Okay."

"Any other arrangements will have to be paid in cash and in advance of any services."

"I understand."

"Good. Your credit card charges have been processed. Gigi should be at your room in approximately one hour."

"That's fine."

"Is there anything else we can do for you?"

"No."

"Then we thank your for your business. I just know you will be pleased with Gigi." Then the line was disconnected.

Henry decided that he needed to take a shower. He went into the bathroom and showered. He put the hotel robe on over his naked body. He stretched out on the bed. His head had just hit the pillow when he heard a knock at his door. He got up and opened it. There was a young woman standing there. "Hi. I'm Gigi."

Henry stood back so that she could enter. She wasn't the same girl that was in the picture, but she was pretty enough. He decided she would serve his purposes.

"I see you have already taken a shower."

"Yes."

She sat down on the bed beside him. She pushed the robe off his thigh and began gently massaging his leg with her well manicured hands. "What's your name, handsome?"

"Robert." Henry lied.

"You're not from around here are you? What part of the South are you from?"

"Mississippi." Henry lied again.

Gigi ran her hand up higher on Henry's leg. She gently brushed his private parts. He felt himself getting excited. "Well, Robert, you have already paid the agency to have me dance for you. I can do that. I will completely strip for you while I dance. You can touch me wherever you want, but that will be all. I would hope that you would give me a generous tip for my dancing."

Henry Mudd had never done anything like this in his entire life. He was a virgin when he married Virginia. He had never been with another woman. He found the prospect of being with this beautiful young woman exciting. He was like a fumbling adolescent. "Okay," he blushed.

"I have a feeling that you're going to want more." With that she opened his robe all the way and began to gently fondle him. "Tell you what, since you are such a good-looking man from Mississippi, I'll do a little something special for you for another hundred and fifty dollars plus a tip."

"Special?" Henry was confused.

Gigi giggled. "Oh, you are an innocent one aren't you? Silly, I'll do oral on you for another hundred and fifty dollars."

Henry flinched. Virginia would never do that for him. When he suggested it, her response was always the same. "Henry, that's disgusting." Then he saw the videos of her doing it on that Frenchman not once, but dozens of times. Now this beautiful young woman was asking to do it for him. Henry felt his arousal heighten at the very thought of it. "Oh, I see you like that idea. Tell you what. For three hundred dollars we'll do everything."

"Okay." Henry couldn't believe that the only word he could come up with was "okay."

"You'll need to pay me first."

Henry opened the drawer in the nightstand next to his bed. He got his money clip and handed her three one hundred dollar bills. "Now I hope that you will also be giving me a nice tip."

Once again the only response Henry could come up with was "okay."

"Before we begin I have to make a telephone call. My body guard is in the lobby. If I don't call him he'll be up here trying to find out if everything is all right." She picked up the telephone and dialed a number. "Everything is fine. I've been paid. I should be down in an hour or less." She then stood and began to undress in front of Henry. Her breasts were full. Henry reached up so that he could feel them. She put her hands over his and encouraged him to massage them. "Oh, that feels so good."

She then finished undressing. "Let's take that robe completely off you." She helped him out of the robe and then gently pushed him back on the bed. She reached into her purse and brought out a small packet. She opened it and rolled the contents onto Henry. She immediately began doing as they had agreed. Henry was excited to watch her take him in that way, but he really couldn't feel anything. He was numb. Nothing was happening. After several minutes she stopped and looked up at him, "What's the matter, Robert? Don't you like this?"

"I just don't feel anything. I mean...I don't know. It's just not working."

She kissed her way up his chest. She kissed his neck. Still, she was unable to arouse him. She scooted over on top of him and looked directly into his face. "Tell you what. Give me another hundred and I'll take the protection off you. I'll bet you'll feel it then."

Henry nodded. He opened the drawer once again. Took out his money clip and gave her another hundred. She got up and put the hundred dollar bill in her purse. She came back to the bed and did as she said she was going to do. It did feel better. It felt much better, but still he could not get the response he wanted.

After a few minutes, he lifted her head off him. "I'm sorry. This has never happened to me before. I don't think it's going to work. I don't know what the problem is. You'd better stop. I'm getting sore. Can we just talk?"

"Sure we can." She moved up beside him and he put his arm around her.

Henry looked over at her. "How long have you been doing this? I mean, you seem to be pretty intelligent. You have great looks. Why are you doing this?"

Gigi giggled and imitated his southern accent, "Why thank you, surh. Let's just say that I'll be graduating in the spring with my Master's Degree in clinical psychology. I won't be doing this after that. I hope to set up a private practice."

"You're a psychologist?"

"I'm psychologist enough right now to have figured out some things about you."

"Oh? Like what?"

She rolled over on her stomach so that she could look at him. "Oh, no you don't. I'm the psychologist so I get to ask the questions."

"Okay. What do you want to ask me?"

She was quiet for a few seconds. Then she took his hand in hers. "Who has hurt you? Someone has hurt you real bad."

Henry was not prepared for the tears that began to roll down his cheeks. She moved so that she could lie on top of him again. Her face was directly above his. She wiped his tears with her hands. "Are you married, Robert?"

Henry nodded.

"Did your wife cheat on you?"

Again, he nodded. "I'm sorry. You really love her don't you?"

"I did, but not any more."

"Then why are you hurting if you don't still love her?"

"I can't even stand to look at her. She's a liar and a whore."

"Careful now," Gigi chuckled. "You're slandering the world's oldest profession. And I just might take that remark personally."

Henry chuckled, "Well, at least you're smart enough to charge. If my addition is correct it's cost me almost seven hundred dollars just to see you naked. My idiot wife was out there giving it away."

"Did she cheat on you with more than one man?"

"I only know of one for sure, but when the trust is gone suspicion sets in. My hunch is that she's cheated on me with others."

"Have you confronted her?"

"Oh, there were a lot of tears. She's so sorry. Please forgive her. She was stupid. She didn't know what she was doing. She still loves me. We can get through this. You know—all the usual clichés."

"Well, I may not know everything just yet, but I don't think that you do that to someone that you love. Have you considered the possibility that she did it in order to hurt you?"

"How could she hurt me if I'd never found out?"

"My guess is that didn't matter to her. She knew she was hurting you. And that's all that mattered."

Henry looked into this beautiful young woman's eyes. "You're going to make one hell of a psychologist. Do you plan on getting married?"

"I hope there's a real nice guy waiting on me out there somewhere. Maybe there's one just like you."

"And would you cheat on him?"

"Here's a little hooker wisdom for you, Robert. You don't cheat on your spouse if you really love them. You only do that if you're trying to hurt them. That's why things didn't work between you and me. You still love her."

"No, I don't."

Her eyes lit up. "Then just who are you protecting?" Then she smiled a knowing smile. "Do you have children?"

He nodded. "Two little girls."

Gigi slapped him gently on the chest. "That's who you're protecting. You're not planning to divorce her, are you?"

"I don't think so. I just can't do that to my girls. I live in a small town. I just don't want everyone knowing what their mother has done."

Gigi sat up in the bed. "Let me understand this. She's the slut and you're the one paying the consequences."

"I think that's the sum of it."

"Wow. Robert, that's really twisted." Gigi pulled a pack of cigarettes out of her purse. "Do you mind if I smoke?"

Henry sat up. He reached for the robe which Gigi had placed at the foot of the bed. "No, I just don't think anything is going to happen tonight. Go ahead and smoke. Would you like a drink?"

"Do you have a beer?"

"I think so." Henry went over to the mini-bar and brought back a beer. He opened it for her. She sat naked on his bed smoking her cigarette and drinking the beer. He stared at her. She was absolutely beautiful. Her body was without flaw. "I don't know what's wrong with me. I would think any man would be happy to possess you, but..."

"Don't worry about it, Robert. You're still hurting. When you've worked through your pain you're going to give some woman a real night of pleasure. And you know what?"

"No. What?"

"Robert, I've been with a lot of men. I know a real catch when I meet one. Your wife is a fool. You may not want to divorce her right now, but one of these days a woman is going to come along that will treat you right. She'll be far too smart to lie to you or to cheat on you. And you won't have to pay for it. She'll happily surrender herself to you."

Gigi stood and started dressing. Henry sat on the side of the bed and watched her. "You sure there's nothing else I can do for you?"

"No...but I want to thank you for all your help. I've really been down on myself. I've felt like such a fool. I've felt so undesirable. I was beginning to see myself as the ugly duckling that no woman would want. You have reassured me." Henry reached for his money clip one more time and gave her a two hundred dollar tip.

Gigi put her arms around Henry's neck and kissed him on the lips. It was a slow passionate kiss. Then she held his face between her two hands and looked him in the eyes. "Robert, you're one of the good guys. Your wife would be a disgrace to my profession. She'd never make it as a hooker." They both giggled as he opened the door for her. That night in a hotel room in Las Vegas, Nevada, Henry Mudd had the first restful night of sleep he'd had in weeks. He slept like a baby. His dreams were not interrupted by any videos of Virginia.

CHAPTER 4

Steele sat staring at the picture time and nature had painted outside his office window. The beautiful old live oak trees stood guard over the burial place of two hundred years of First Church history. The magnolias had Spanish moss dripping like icicles on a Christmas tree from their dark green leaves. He stared at the tower pointing heavenward on top of First Church. He was lost in his thoughts and the majesty of all that lay before him. "I didn't hear you come in, Father Austin."

He turned to see that his secretary, Crystal had opened the door between their offices. "I came in early to make a telephone call."

"Well, you have a bunch of telephone messages here." She handed him a stack of pink telephone slips that were at least one half inch thick." These are all the same. They're from members of the parish, community leaders, other pastors, teachers in First Church School. They're all the same. They're begging you not to leave First Church. I think the rumor that you might leave is the talk of the town."

Steele took the slips from her and quickly thumbed through a few of them. He smiled, "Well, I guess they're going to get their way."

Crystal quickly sat down in the chair opposite Steele's desk. A big smile crossed her face, "So you're going to stay?"

He nodded.

"Oh, Father Austin. You've made my day. I really didn't want to look for another job. Are you sure? I mean, this is a really difficult parish. They haven't been very nice to you."

"It's all right, Crystal. I really think I've made the right decision. There are difficult personalities in every parish. The good thing is that at least I know who they are here. And I even think I've won all but a few of them over."

"I hope so. How are you going to let the parish know?"

"I was just sitting here thinking about that very thing. I'd thought about sending out a letter. We may still do that, but I think I want to tell them myself. I'm going to make the announcement this Sunday in church."

Crystal smiled again. "I think that's a wonderful idea." Then she glanced down at the fax in her hand and her smile disappeared. "Oh, I almost forgot. This came early this morning. It may cause you to think that you've made the wrong decision. After you read it, you may want to change your mind."

Steele reached for the fax. It was from Bishop Petersen. He let out a low whistle, "What does he want now?"

Crystal stood and started walking toward the door. "I think I'll leave you to read it for yourself. I glanced through it. It very well could spoil your day. I'm so sorry. Let me know if you want to send a response after you've read it." She closed the door.

Steele began reading the fax which was on the Bishop's letterhead.
Reverend Austin,

This is a most difficult letter for this Bishop to write one of the priests in his charge. However, I take my responsibilities to care for all the people in this Diocese seriously. While this letter is most unpleasant for me to write, I would be remiss not to do so. Yesterday, I received a fax from your Senior Warden. It contained a new Letter of Agreement that your Vestry has voted to offer you if you will stay at First Church. I was both shocked and repulsed by its contents.

Reverend Austin, there is no other way to say this. You have blackmailed the good people of First Church! Your greed has led them to offer you a compensation package that is absolutely shameful. The compensation you've swindled them into offering exceeds that of this Bishop by several thousands of dollars! It's even more egregious when it is compared to the total budgets of half the congregations in this Diocese. Your proposed salary and appurtenances exceed the total operating budgets of each of those congregations. Mister Austin, this is outrageous! If you are successful in your efforts to convince the good men on the Vestry at First Church to persist with this agreement, you must know that I will only sign it under protest and with much disappointment in you.

Beyond your greed, my disappointment in you and your ministry in this Diocese continues to grow. You, sir, have chosen not to exercise a collegial ministry with your fellow priests. You have chosen to act like the Lone Ranger with your faithful companion,

Tonto, i.e., Horace Drummond, by your side. You have let down this Bishop and your brother priests. The Rector of the largest parish in our Diocese should be active in the counsels of this church. You have chosen to participate in none of them. Instead, you have persisted in your divisive ministry of controversy. You continue to squander the good funds of the people of First Church on your pet projects that would best be left to the United Way or the Salvation Army.

This latest Letter of Agreement has only confirmed my worst suspicions about you. You have entered the priesthood to serve no one but yourself. You accepted the call to First Church because you saw the wealth of her treasure and you continue to plot a methodology of using that treasure to feed your own greed.

I conclude this letter with yet one more godly admonition. You need to know that I am fully aware of your efforts to undermine the ministry of this Bishop. You have violated your oath of ordination to be obedient to your Bishop and support him in his ministry. I refuse to sit back and allow you to continue to undermine me. In my very next address to the Diocesan Convention, I plan to name the names of those who are actively seeking to unseat me as Bishop. Your name, sir, will be one of those that I will read publicly!

I seriously doubt that any of this will bring about a change in your behavior. You are determined to follow your path of self-destruction. The only thing I can do is remember you in my prayers. So that you will fully realize the seriousness of this communication, I am both sending it to you by fax and special delivery through the postal service.

In God's Service, I am

The Right Reverend Rufus Petersen
Bishop of Savannah

Steele sat in disbelief. He then read the letter through a second time. He reached to pick up the telephone and call Randi. He was going to share it with her and then call Charles Gerard in San Antonio and let him know that they'd changed their minds. They would be coming to St.

Jude's. His thoughts were interrupted when Crystal knocked and opened the door. "Do you want to respond to that fax?"

Steele sat back in his chair. "No, I think some letters don't deserve a response. This is one of them."

She nodded. "Do you have a minute? There's a young man in the waiting room asking for help. Doctor Drummond is not here today. Normally, I would ask him to come back tomorrow and meet with him. But Father Austin, I'm really worried about this guy. If you have a few minutes, I think you should see him."

Steele saw the concern on her face. She had become a pro at screening most of the transients. He trusted her to be able to screen those that needed immediate attention. "Anything I have to do can wait. Go ahead and send him in."

Crystal opened the door and a teenage boy entered. "Father Austin, this is Bud. Bud, this is Father Austin."

"Let's sit over here on the couch, Bud." Crystal shut the door. The young man took a seat. He glanced at Steele and then dropped his head to look at the floor. Steele studied him. He estimated that he could be as young as fourteen and no older than sixteen. He was slim, but well muscled. He was obviously no stranger to the gym. He was wearing a skin tight tee shirt and jeans. The front portion of his long dark hair had been bleached blonde. Steele studied him further. In spite of his toned body, there was something fragile about him. Steele glanced over at his hands. He had several cheap-looking rings on his fingers. There was a leather bracelet around his left wrist. Then Steele found the clue he was looking for. He detected the remnants of red fingernail polish on his fingernails. That completed the picture in Steele's mind. "Bud, are you gay?"

Bud glanced up at Steele and nodded. Tears flooded his eyes.

"Do your parents know?"

Bud blurted, "That's the problem. They found out. Then they threw me out of the house. They told me not to come back until I'd made up my mind that I was going to be a real man. Father, I don't have any place to go. I don't have a home. I don't have a family. I don't know what I'm going to do."

"Where are you from?"

"Brunswick."

Steele knew that Brunswick, Georgia was near the Florida—Georgia border. "How long ago did your parents throw you out?"

"Two weeks ago."

"Were you using drugs, Bud?"

"No, it was nothing like that. I don't even smoke cigarettes. I've only had a couple of beers in my entire life."

"They threw you out because you're gay?"

Again, Bud nodded. "My mother walked in on me with one of my friends."

"Walked in on you?"

"Yeah, we were...you know. We love each other."

Steele nodded. "Where's your friend?"

"My mom became hysterical and started calling us names. Kevin, that's my friend, got dressed and ran out of my house. She called my dad at work and he came home. He beat me with a belt real bad. My mom threw a few of my clothes in a bag and they threw me out of the house. They told me not to come back until I had repented of my sinful ways."

"Did you go to Kevin's?"

"Yeah, but the police were there when I got to his house."

Steele was surprised. "The police?"

"Yeah, my mom had called Kevin's dad. When Kevin got home, his dad started beating him with a baseball bat or a club or something like that. Kevin ran into the kitchen. He was trying to get away from him. He blocked the kitchen door, but his father broke it down. He used to be a football player. He's a really big guy. Kevin isn't. Kevin is short and thin like me. Anyway, Kevin took a knife out of the drawer and stabbed his dad with it. It didn't kill him and I think he's going to be all right, but his mom called the police and they arrested Kevin."

"Wow, you've really been living a nightmare."

Tears dropped down Bud's cheeks. "I had no place to go so I hitched a ride over here. I'm trying to get up to Atlanta."

"How long have you been in Falls City?"

"A week."

"Where have you been staying?"

"I've stayed underneath the Falls Bridge with some of the homeless most of the nights. They've been really helpful. They told me about you and this church. They also told me about your Soup Kitchen, so I've been able to eat." Bud blushed a bright red.

"Is there something else you need to tell me?"

Bud studied Steele's face. "You know Falls Park?"

"Yes."

"You know they have some public bathrooms down there?"

"Yes, I know that they're there."

"A couple of times I've been able to service some of the closeted married guys down there. They've given me money and paid for me to have a couple of nights in a cheap hotel."

"That's really dangerous, Bud. You know that, don't you?"

"I know, but Father Austin, what am I supposed to do? I don't have any place to live."

Steele's heart went out to him. He'd read news stories about teenagers being disowned by their parents because they'd discovered they were gay, but this was his first personal encounter with one. "Have you met other teens like you out there on the streets?"

"Father Austin, they're everywhere. There are six of us that eat together at your Soup Kitchen."

Steele was shocked. "Six?"

"Oh, I'll bet you have more than that right here in Falls City."

Steele sat back. A plan started unfolding in his mind. "Bud, I want to help you. I'm going to help you right now, but I want to help you and other young people like you on a more permanent basis."

"Are you going to try to turn me straight?"

Steele chuckled, "Bud, you and I both know that won't work, will it?"

Bud smiled. "I don't think so. Father Austin, look at me. Do you really think there's a closet anywhere that I could hide in?"

Steele chuckled again. "Do you have any money, Bud?"

Bud reached into the front pocket in his jeans and brought out a handful of change. He quickly counted it. "I have sixty-eight cents."

"Have you been eating all your meals in the Soup Kitchen?"

"I've eaten as many as I could over there, but I've also done a little panhandling. Some of the homeless under the bridge have shared their food with me. And then...well...I told you about the park."

Steele stood and went over to the intercom on his desk. "Crystal, will you get Skipper Hodges over at the shelter on the line for me? Then I want you to get the bookkeeper to cut a check for fifty dollars out of my

Discretionary Fund. Make it out to cash and have her go over to the bank and bring the money back in small bills. Tell her to note on the memo that it's for assistance. Bud and I will be down in the school cafeteria having an early lunch. You'll be able to find us there."

Steele waited by the phone for just a minute. "Father Austin, I have Mister Hodges on line 67."

Steele pushed the blinking line button. "Hey Skipper, I have a young man in my office that needs a place to sleep for the next few days. Don't you have a room over there that you reserve just for teens?"

"We do, Father Austin. We have one room for teenagers. We've learned that it's best to keep them separate from the rest of the population. But Father, it's full. I can't take another."

"Oh no, how many do you have over there right now?"

"We have four bunk beds in the room but they're all occupied."

"Wow! You've got eight homeless teens sleeping over there right now?"

"Father Austin, if I had the room I could house over twenty a night."

"I'm going to want to talk to you more about that later on, but do you have any ideas as to how I could find this young man in my office a place to stay?"

"Father, may I ask? Is he gay?"

"Yes, but does that matter?"

Skipper chuckled, "No, it was just a hunch. At this location the overwhelming majority of the teens are on the streets because they are gay or lesbian. When I was working at the center out in Arizona it seemed like the primary reason teens were kicked out by their parents was drugs."

"Interesting."

"Since it's you, Father Austin, I'll tell you what I'll do. Have your young man come on over. I'll put a cot in the middle of the room. Just don't tell the fire marshal. It'll be a bit crowded, but we can only keep him three days. That's our maximum stay per week."

"Skipper, I really appreciate it. I'll try to work on a longer term solution. I really appreciate you and all that you are doing. Thanks again for the help. I'll talk to you soon."

Steele returned to his chair opposite the couch. "Bud, can you come back to see me tomorrow? I want my associate, Doctor Drummond, to meet you. I think the two of us might just be able to do something long term for kids like you that have no place to go."

Bud sat straight up on the couch. "What kind of doctor is he?"

Steele smiled, "Don't worry. He's a priest just like me. He's really good at coming up with long-term solutions for the problems that people are experiencing."

"What did you have in mind?"

"I need a week or maybe longer to work on that. I have some thoughts, but it's going to take a little time. In the meantime, I need you to promise me several things."

"Shoot."

"First, you stay out of Falls Park. Second, no more servicing any closeted married guys. Third, no unsafe sex with anyone. Fourth, no alcohol, no drugs, no criminal activity of any kind. And fifth, you secure a part-time job, even if it's just at a fast food restaurant. If everything works out for you here in Falls City, we'll have to get you enrolled in school."

"Not a problem. You have my word." Bud looked relieved. He smiled at Steele. "Thank you, Father Austin. The homeless under the bridge told me that you were my only hope in Falls City. You know they have a name for you, don't you?"

"No, I didn't know that. What do they call me?"

Bud's body shook with laughter. "They call you Father T."

"Father T?"

"Yeah, you know…like Mister T on the old television show."

Now it was Steele's turn to let the laughter pour out of him. "I don't even have a gold necklace. But you know what, Bud? I want to thank you for coming to see me. I was having some second thoughts about a major decision in my life. You have just helped me make peace with the fact that I've made the right decision. I'm doing exactly what God wants me to do. Now let's go get some lunch."

CHAPTER 5

*M*ildred's Café is a local favorite for the longtime residents of Falls City. *Mildred's* has been in the same location at the edge of downtown for over fifty years. It's in a nondescript building with booths, tables and chairs that should have been replaced years ago. There's a counter for those who are dining alone or just want to be able to converse with the waitresses while they eat. *Just Like Mom's* is printed underneath the café name. Chicken Fried Steak with lots of flour gravy, fried okra, and collard greens is a dinner favorite for the locals. Mildred serves that with deep fried cornbread sticks that leave a lot to be desired. The standing joke is—"Don't drop one of those cornbread sticks on your foot or it'll break it." That always brings a round of knowing chuckles. Of course, diners are given a large glass of sweet tea with their meal. Mildred mixes her sweet tea with one part sugar and two parts tea.

The crowd from the 7:30 Tuesday morning service at First Church has habitually gathered at *Mildred's* for breakfast after the service for decades. Breakfast at *Mildred's* was a special treat. Cheese-garlic grits served with fluffy flour biscuits and Country Ham is the most frequently ordered item on the breakfast menu. Country Ham dates back to the days before refrigeration was a possibility. Mildred takes great pride in the way she prepares her Country Ham. She first has a ham cured and then soaked in saltwater brine. Then it's smoked. It's tightly wrapped in a cloth bag and left hanging in a smokehouse behind the café for several months. When the cloth is cut away from the ham itself, it's often covered with mold. The mold is cut away and the ham is then soaked in water. This removes some of the salt and adds moisture to the ham itself. Normally, people only soak their ham for a few hours. Not Mildred. She likes to soak her ham for several days. She soaks her hams in a cooler so there is less of a chance that bacteria will grow on them. She also changes the water every day. Once she determines the ham is ready for cooking she has it rinsed off one last time. This removes any bacteria that did develop and the coating of salt that might remain. Then she slowly cooks it on a grill.

Most people cook their Country Ham in the oven. Mildred prefers to use a charcoal grill with smoked wood chips. While it cooks on the grill, Mildred instructs that it be basted frequently with her secret ingredient. People had tried for years to discover her secret ingredient. Last year she fired one of her cooks. It was not a happy dismissal. He decided not to go quietly into the dark night of unemployment. In order to get even with Mildred, he told everyone he knew that her secret ingredient was soda pop. It seems she bastes her Country Ham with RC Cola. She continues to baste it even while it's grilling. The Country Ham has to grill for up to four hours. Only Mildred determines when it's ready. She does that the old fashioned way, just like your mother. She gives it the taste test.

Some of the regulars at *Mildred's* have an inside joke about her cooking. They wink and quip, "Mildred needs to change the motto on her sign out front. Instead of *Just Like Mom's.* The sign should ask *is she trying to feed you or kill you?"*

Virginia Mudd was one of but a handful of ladies on the First Church Altar Guild that had been authorized to set up services. She was the youngest woman on the Guild by far that could perform this function. Most women had to serve in lower capacities on the Altar Guild for decades before they were trained to set up services. Virginia's prominent position in the greater Falls City society dictated that she be a singular exception.

Virginia had been awakened early. She was glad that Henry was out of town. Even though they no longer shared a marriage bed, she did not want him to know about her morning routine the past few days. She had been waking up nauseated. She seemed to be fine once she was able to empty her stomach. Then…she had noticed that her breasts were tender. She knew the symptoms. Her worst fears were being realized. She was hoping against hope that she was wrong. Still, she was terrified.

She arrived at the chapel forty-five minutes before the service was to begin. This was in keeping with the specific directions that had been placed in the First Church Altar Guild Manual close to two hundred years ago. She was putting on her Altar Guild smock and chapel cap when Martha Dexter opened the Sacristy door. Virginia had come to despise that woman. She feared that Martha might have discovered her affair with Jacque. At the very least, she believed Martha held some suspicions. Martha's husband, Howard, was on the museum board where Jacque had been the director. Martha was often volunteering at the museum. Virginia feared that she may have seen her with Jacque. Virginia had chastised herself over and over for taking the risk of meeting Jacque at the museum for some of their liaisons. She should have known better.

"Good morning, Virginia." Martha cooed. "It's so distressing about the Bishop, don't you think?"

Virginia shook her head. "Good Morning, Martha. What are you talking about? I haven't heard anything about the Bishop."

"Oh…I guess the word hasn't gotten around yet. My Howard got a telephone call from the Diocesan House early this morning. I guess they're just calling the Senior Wardens and the clergy."

Virginia busied herself with taking the communion vessels out of the chapel safe. "Is the Bishop ill?"

"Oh, Virginia, it's all just so distressing. We need to make sure that the reader has him on the prayer list for the Prayers of the People this morning."

"Did he have an accident?"

"No, Virginia. The Bishop had a heart attack. I guess it was a really bad one. He's in critical condition at the Medical Center in Savannah. They don't know if he's going to live or die."

Virginia stopped her work to look at Martha. "That's just terrible. He's such a godly man. Why is it that all the bad things seem to happen to the really good people?"

"I don't know. I have no explanation for it. Think about all the troublemakers in the world. They just keep on going without any grief or pain and then you take a saint like Bishop Petersen…" Martha shook her head and resumed setting up the altar. "It just doesn't make any sense."

They worked quietly until all was in readiness. Then the two of them continued to stand in silence in the Sacristy until the priest presiding at the morning service could arrive. Martha broke the silence, "Virginia, I guess you heard that we had to fire the Museum Director."

"Yes, I read it in the newspaper."

"I owe you and Henry an apology. If I'd known that he was the type of man that would have an adulterous relationship with another man's wife…" She stopped and took a deep breath. "Well, if I'd known he was so rotten I would never have insisted that you invite him to your dinner party for the Bishop."

"No apology is needed, Martha. What is done is done."

Martha moved so that she could stand directly in front of Virginia. She stared into her eyes. Her two front teeth protruded as she smiled a knowing smile. "You know he was having a sexual relationship with a married woman right here in Falls City?"

Virginia turned away and pretended to dust the top of the Sacristy counter. "I think I had heard something about that, but it was not reported in the newspaper story."

Martha was not to be dissuaded. "Can I ask you something, Virginia?"

Virginia Mudd felt a chill run up her spine. "You can ask me anything you want."

"Well, is everything all right with you and Henry?"

Virginia spun around to look at Martha. She pretended surprise by quickly placing her hand over her heart. "Why, Martha Dexter, what would cause you to ask such a question? Everything is just perfect between my Henry and me. You know he's out of town this week on business. He's in Las Vegas."

"No, I didn't know. It's just that several of us had observed that your seating arrangement at church has been modified."

Virginia gave Martha a questioning look. "Modified? What on earth do you mean?"

"Well, you and Henry have always sat next to each other. He always has his arm around you. The last few weeks you have put the girls in between you. Are you sure that everything is all right between the two of you?"

Virginia pretended a chuckle. "Oh, Martha, the girls don't want to sit by any of these new people that the Rector keeps crowding into our church. Our pew is so crowded there is simply not enough room for any of us to take a deep breath. You have noticed that these new people just keep coming. I don't know who they are or where he finds them. That Rector has got to be brought under control. I hope your husband is talking to him about cutting back on his new member recruitment program."

Martha didn't answer. She just stood staring at Virginia with her knowing smile masked only by her two protruding teeth. Virginia was saved when Doctor Drummond arrived. "Good morning, ladies. It's a beautiful morning isn't it? Will the two of you be joining us for breakfast at *Mildred's* following the service?"

They both smiled and nodded. Virginia resolved that she was not going to give Martha any more opportunities to cross-examine her. She would not be going to breakfast at Mildred's.

CHAPTER 6

Rufus Petersen felt someone touch his hand. He opened his eyes. The nurse was checking his pulse. "You awake, Bishop?" He struggled to get his eyes to focus on her face. His mouth and throat were so dry. "May I have a glass of water?"

"No, not just yet, but I'll wipe your lips with an ice cube."

Rufus shook his head. "I want some water."

The nurse turned to leave the room. "I'll ask your doctor. He'll be by to see you in a few minutes." Then she left him to his discomfort and his thoughts.

Rufus looked around his room. It was filled with large arrangements of flowers. He struggled to sit up in his bed. Just then there was a knock at his door. A man wearing a long white coat with a stethoscope around his neck entered. He was followed by the nurse that had previously taken his pulse. "Bishop Petersen," he extended his hand for the Bishop to shake. "I'm Doctor Mitchell. I'm the cardiologist that was on duty when EMS brought you into the hospital."

Rufus didn't think the man looked old enough to be a doctor of any kind. He had blonde hair and deep blue eyes. He was tall and razor thin. Rufus nodded at him. "Bishop, you really gave us all quite a scare, but I want you to know that you're a mighty lucky man. You had not just one, but two coronary events. By the time they got you to the hospital, your condition was critical. Do you understand what I'm saying to you?"

Rufus struggled to speak. "I'm just so thirsty. Can't I have something to drink?"

The doctor turned his head and nodded at the nurse. "Let him have a couple of swallows of room temperature water. Let's see how he does."

The nurse approached his bed with the glass. "I'm going to raise your bed up just a bit." She pushed the button on the control panel on his bed railing. He felt the bed lifting him into a semi-seated position. She brought the cup to his lips. "Slow now, let's do this real slow. Just take one small swallow at a time."

Rufus followed her instructions. He was able to drink without any difficulty. "Thank you." He laid his head back on his pillow so he could look at the doctor. The doctor was now sitting on the edge of his bed.

"Bishop, I put four stints in your heart. Do you understand why I would need to do that?"

Rufus felt himself growing impatient. He wanted to shout at the doctor, "Why are you treating me like an idiot? I've been in and out of hospitals for forty years ministering to the sick and dying. Of course, I know why you'd have to put a stint in a heart vessel. Who the hell do you think has been burying all you doctor's mistakes?" Instead of yelling, Rufus just nodded.

The doctor persisted. "Four of your coronary arteries were blocked. One of them was almost completely closed. I'm surprised that you hadn't had some symptoms or an event before now."

"Why the hell does he keep calling it *an event?*" Rufus wanted to shout at the top of his lungs. He was really growing impatient. "I didn't have an event, you punk. I had a heart attack. It sounds like I had two of them. Now just tell me, am I going to live or die?" Rufus realized that the doctor was still talking. "...because of the severity of the attacks and your overall health, I believed that the stints were our best option. Do you have any questions?"

Rufus tried to speak but the best he could get out was a hoarse whisper. "What next?"

"Well, you're going to be in here a few more days. We're going to start you out on liquids and then move you to solids. We need to keep an eye on you."

"And...my prognosis?"

"Bishop, an awfully lot of that depends on you. Our cardiac rehab nurse is going to be coming up to talk to you about some of the changes you've simply got to make in your life."

"Changes...what kind of changes?"

"Diet, exercise, avoiding stress, weight loss, alcohol, smoking..." he smiled. "Well, she'll go into all the details, but as your doctor I'm telling you that I've done all I can do for you surgically. There's no reason that you can't live a productive life for many more years with the stints."

He stood, "Do you have any other questions?"

Rufus shook his head. "Not right now."

"Are you experiencing any pain?"

Rufus had not even thought about pain. "No, not really. I'm just a little sore and quite weak. When can I have something to eat?"

"Bishop, first liquids for a day or so and then some soft solids will follow. I'm not going to discharge you until you're back up on your feet. I'll check back on you later in the day." He walked toward the door, stopped and turned to look back at him. "Bishop, I cannot overemphasize the importance of listening to every detail the cardiac nurse is going to discuss with you. Your life is literally in your hands from now on." With that he turned and walked out the door. The nurse followed behind him.

Rufus lay in silence. He closed his eyes. With his eyes closed he could see the face of his mother. It all started to come back to him. He remembered the entire thing. He replayed it in his mind. Was it a dream? No, he told himself. It wasn't a dream. It was just too real. The entire experience was so real. He remembered being outside of his body. He remembered watching EMS work on him. Then he remembered the ringing and the swirling lights. His mother was not a dream. She was no vision. He really did see her.

The nurse interrupted his thoughts. She brought a tray in and placed it on his bedside table. She then pushed the button to lift his bed even higher. She fluffed his pillows. "The doctor wants to see just how you might do with some broth." She pulled his bedside table across the bed in front of him. "Can you feed yourself?"

Rufus nodded. "I've been doing it for years."

"Well, all the same, I'm going to stay and see how the first few swallows go down."

Rufus picked up the spoon and dipped it in the bowl. The warm liquid felt good on his lips and tongue. Surprisingly, it actually tasted quite good. "Okay, I'll leave you for now, but if you need anything, push your call button."

After she had left, Rufus finished the bowl of broth and pushed the tray table away from his bed. He pushed the button on his bed and lowered his head. Thoughts of his mother passed before him once again. He was convinced now beyond a shadow of a doubt that his experience had been real. He had seen his mother. He had talked to his mother. Then it hit him. He realized that he had died and been brought back to this side of the veil. He heard her words once again. "Rufus, I'm disappointed in you. You need to be a different kind of person. You need to do better." Her words echoed over and over in his mind. He put his hands to his ears and squeezed his eyes tightly shut. He couldn't get the sound of her voice to stop. Her words were burning themselves into his soul. He felt himself on the verge of breaking. And then the Bishop of Savannah relaxed. The tears flowed out of him. His body shook with the grief.

CHAPTER 7

K nock, knock." Steele looked up from his desk to see his associate, Horace Drummond, enter. "You got a minute? I need to talk with you."

"Sure, come on in."

Horace shut the door behind him. "You know that the word is out that you're going to stay with us here at First Church."

Steele nodded. "Yeah, I figured as much."

"I think a formal announcement of some sort is in order."

"I'd planned on doing it this Sunday from the pulpit. I thought perhaps I would then follow up with a letter."

'That sounds good to me. Are you going to try to explain just why you've chosen to stay?"

"I'm planning to make a stab at it."

"You realize that your antagonists are already accusing you of blackmailing the Vestry?"

Steele was quiet for several minutes. He studied his dear friend's face. "You know, Horace. Sometimes I'm just so naïve. I didn't ask the Vestry for anything. They offered to match the package in San Antonio."

"I know that and all your friends and supporters know it. You need to leave money out of it and focus on the real reason you chose to stay."

Steele opened his desk drawer and shoved the letter Bishop Petersen had mailed him across the desk for Horace to read. "He first sent this by fax. Then this copy arrived in the mail."

Horace read the letter. His eyes widened and he grunted several times. "This has got to be one of the ugliest letters a priest has ever received from a Bishop."

"Look at the date and time of the fax. He wrote it right before he had his heart attack."

"Well, if this letter becomes public, it's not going to help you here or in the Diocese. Since his heart attack, he has the sympathy of this entire parish. Even the folks that don't like him are feeling sorry for him. Have you heard any more from the Diocesan Office about his prognosis?"

"His secretary has been really good about calling with a daily update. It appears that he's making progress. He's scheduled now to go home this weekend."

Steele took the letters back from Horace. "I haven't even shown them to Randi. You and Crystal are the only two people that have seen them here at First Church."

Horace sat in silence. Steele studied his dear friend's face once again. "What are you trying not to tell me, Horace?"

"Am I that transparent?"

"I know you have a really good heart and something is bothering you. So out with it."

Horace's voice was just above a whisper. "What are you going to do about Judith Idle?"

This time it was Steele's turn to be silent. After several minutes he uttered in a low voice, "I don't know."

"Steele, she's relentless. Not only does she continue to argue that you framed the administrator, but her husband is equally venomous. They insist you are stealing money from First Church. They tell the same to anyone that will listen. I've told you before that those two people are the most dangerous enemies you have in this parish. They've fooled most everyone into believing that had they been alive at the time, Jesus would have hand-picked them to be among the apostles."

"I know that they're out there with their accusations, but I just don't believe any thinking person will listen to them."

"But that's the point. Most people don't think when it comes to a juicy bit of gossip. They just enjoy it and pass it on."

"I know that you're right. I have a proposal from her that she start a new prayer group here in the parish."

Horace shook his head and let out a moan. "Leading a prayer group will give her a new pulpit from which she can proclaim her gospel of hate. Leaders of prayer groups also get to wrap themselves in a mantle of holiness. It will only increase the credibility of her attacks on you."

"What do you suggest?"

"I honestly don't know. If you fire her, you'll have to deal with her husband, Elmer. My understanding is that he's already started a campaign to be elected Senior Warden at the Annual Meeting."

Steele's eyes widened. "I hadn't heard that one."

"It's just bad business to have a staff member with a spouse on the Vestry. There's one more thing you need to know."

"Go ahead."

"Judy and Elmer have become bosom buddies with your old arch enemy Ned Boone."

"I thought maybe Ned was pulling in his horns. I mean, we both agreed on opposing the School Board's efforts to separate the school from the parish. I thought maybe we could have a fresh start."

Horace shook his head. "Steele, the Idles and Ned have been seen at the Country Club having hushed conversations. You met our house boy, remember?"

"Yes, I remember him."

"He knows a couple of the waiters at the Country Club. He says that they told him they're whispering about a plan for getting rid of you if you don't accept the call to go to San Antonio."

Steele shrugged. "Horace, I just don't know what I can do about it. I think I've made the right decision for me and for First Church. I'm not going to let the Idles and Ned Boone keep us from doing that which I believe God wants us to do in this place."

"Just know that there are a lot of people in this parish that are really happy that you're staying. We're ready to help you. You only need to let us know what you want us to do."

Steele smiled, "Thanks, I really appreciate that. Let's change subjects. What do you think about Bud?"

Horace chuckled. "You mean our new boarder."

Steele was astonished. "Your what?"

Horace roared with laughter. "I spent a morning with Bud. That young man has really been through it. While I was meeting with him, Almeda called me. I told her a little bit about him and she asked me to bring him home for lunch."

"You're kidding."

"Steele, that woman continually surprises me. Well, to make a long story short, Almeda fell in love with the young man. She insisted that he stay with us in one of our guest rooms. Steele, they've become best friends. She took him shopping for some new clothes. Then he took her shopping." Horace paused in order to laugh some more. "Steele, Almeda has a new girlfriend."

With that both men broke out into laughter. Then Horace got a puzzled look on his face. "Steele, she did say something that really confused me."

"Oh?"

"Yeah, last night before we went to bed, I asked her just why she was so sympathetic to Bud's plight. Then she said something that really confused me."

"What was that?"

"She said that she'd always had a soft spot in her heart for gay men. What do you think she meant by that, Steele?"

Steele shrugged and smiled. "I guess you'll have to ask her."

CHAPTER 8

Henry Mudd woke up in a cold sweat. He was nauseated. The nightmares and cold sweats had become a familiar part of his sleep pattern the past few weeks. Tonight's desperate dream had been the same one that he had repeatedly since discovering his wife's infidelity. They were at a large party at the Magnolia Club. They were standing together talking to a mutual friend. Then, without notice, Virginia disappears. Henry begins a desperate search to find her. His feet and legs feel like they are made of lead. It takes all his strength to move them. People keep coming up to him, smiling and laughing. They want to talk to him, but their interruptions are unwanted. He needs to find Virginia.

The panic sets in as everything and everyone in the club ballroom goes into slow motion. He tries to yell for her, but no sound will come out of his mouth. His heart begins to beat faster. Panic envelopes him. Frantically, he moves about the ballroom. Where has she gone? His worst fears flash before him. He opens the doors to the conference rooms surrounding the grand ball room. He struggles up the stairs to look out at the crowd from the balcony. He forces his legs to carry him down the stairs to the bar. She can't be found.

He's now sick to his stomach. Virginia has disappeared. He struggles to loosen his tie. He removes his jacket. He exits the club in order to look for her in the parking lot. The cool night air feels good to him. Painfully he moves from car to car to see if she is in any of them. Then a scream forms in his throat as he peers into the window of an unfamiliar automobile. There is his wife with her face between that Frenchman's naked legs. His entire body convulses with the vomit spewing from his mouth. That's when he wakes, shaking, sick to his stomach, and in a cold sweat. His pajamas are soaked. His bed sheets are wet with perspiration.

Henry strained to look at the clock on the bedside table. It was right at 5:30 in the morning. That particular nightmare had become his constant bedtime companion. He lay reliving the dream. The problem with the dream was that it was grounded in reality. He could remember a time when he and Virginia were never separated at a party. She was always at his side. They were a couple. They would spend the entire evening together. They would walk from person to person holding hands. He would cuddle her in his arm when they talked with others. A few months ago that all changed. Virginia really did begin to disappear at parties. At first he didn't think anything of it. Then he became suspicious. Where had she gone? He would ask her. "Oh, I guess we got separated in the crowd." Her response was always the same, but she never reappeared until it was almost time to go home.

Henry went into the bathroom and removed his pajamas. He used a towel to wipe the perspiration from his body. He reached into the dresser and brought out dry underwear and a dry tee shirt. He pulled the blanket up over the damp sheet on his bed and lay down. His pillows were damp so he turned them over. Henry lay in the darkness lost in his thoughts. New York flashed before him. Virginia had wanted to go with him a few weeks ago. He assured her that he would be taking depositions all day and would not be free until later in the evening. That didn't seem to bother her. She would go along to shop and just do New York City.

Virginia told him that she'd gotten a list of restaurants from a friend. So each day she would eat lunch in a different eatery. She was excited about the trip. When he left her in the hotel each morning she was getting dressed for her day. He had felt guilty about leaving her on her own in such a big city. She didn't seem to mind. Now he remembered that she was actually excited about each of her days on her own. Then a light dawned in the back of Henry's mind. He sat up in the bed. He realized that she was not afraid to be in the big city because she was not there alone. She was there to meet that Frenchman. The two of them probably spent the day in his hotel room. Henry hated himself for being so stupid. He loved her. He trusted her. He was a fool! He whispered, "Oh hell, even if she wasn't there to meet the Frenchman, the slut was probably just picking up men around the city for afternoon quickies." Henry hated himself. He hated her for what she had done to their marriage—to him—and to their children. But each time he had the dream, he woke and another piece of her pattern of adultery would fall into place.

Just then he heard something from Virginia's bathroom. It was a familiar sound. He rose from the bed and quietly walked across the hall to her bedroom. He opened the door. Virginia was in the master bathroom. The sounds were undeniable. He decided to wait. In a few minutes, the door opened. Virginia let out a low squeal when she saw Henry standing in her dark bedroom. "You startled me. I didn't know you were there."

"What's going on, Virginia?"

"Oh, it must have been something that I ate last night."

"Stop it, Virginia. Can you just stop lying to me for five minutes?"

Virginia put her hand over her heart. "Why, Henry, what on earth are you talking about? I just have a small case of food poisoning."

"Damn it, Virginia. You've become so used to lying to me that you can't stop yourself. You insist on lying to me when telling me the truth would serve you so much better."

"Henry, I'm confused. What on earth are you talking about?"

"Okay, Virginia. We'll do it your way. First, you don't have food poisoning. You've got morning sickness." Henry stared at her breasts. "Look at your breasts, Virginia." He reached out and squeezed one of her breasts.

"Ouch, Henry; they're tender."

"Exactly!"

"It's just my time of the month."

"Virginia, I'm only going to say this once. You're pregnant. I know it and you know it. Now let's get one thing very clear. The only reason that you're still living under the same roof with me is those two little girls sleeping down the hall. If it weren't for them, you'd be the laughing stock of this town. You'd have no friends. It's taking everything in my power to keep from branding you with a big scarlet 'A' and throwing you out there for the gossiping dogs to ravage."

Virginia started crying. "I've told you I'm so sorry. Why can't you forgive me?"

Henry smirked. "Forgive you?" He took a deep breath. "Virginia, don't even think about bringing your French bastard into this house. I don't know what you're going to do, but you will not bring that frog's child into my house. Do I make myself clear?"

Virginia wiped her eyes and nodded.

"If you have to go away for a year or so, then do it. I'll cover for you with the girls and the community." Henry shot her a disgusted look. "But Virginia, I'm growing tired of lying for you. I'm not sure just how long I can keep on doing it. You have broken my heart into a thousand pieces. You have completely destroyed this home. And you have humiliated me beyond words. Do not count on me keeping your secrets forever. There's a reason that they stoned adulterous wives in the Bible. Believe me, I've finally figured out just why they did that. If you do one more thing to test my patience, I promise you that I'll throw the very first stone myself."

Virginia began crying all the harder and ran for her bed. She lay down and pulled the covers up to her chin. Henry stood glaring at her. Then, he turned and walked out of the room they had shared for their entire married life. He closed the door behind him. He walked down the hall and opened the doors to his daughter's rooms. He stood at each of their doors watching them sleep. He whispered a prayer of thanksgiving to God for them. He resolved again that he would not let their mother disgrace them. He returned to what had now become his bedroom. He turned on the shower. The hot water poured over his body. Life had dealt Henry Mudd an ugly hand. He was determined to play it as a Christian and a gentleman. He was determined to play it in such a way that his beautiful little girls would never have to suffer because of their mother's sins.

CHAPTER 9

After the reading of the Gospel appointed for the morning, the crucifer, torches, verger, and deacon processed back to the altar while the organist improvised a fanfare on the organ. Steele climbed the pulpit steps and stood watching the Gospel procession return to the sanctuary. When all had returned to their places, the organist ceased to play. Steele blessed himself with the sign of the cross before beginning his sermon. He opened his mouth to speak but he was interrupted by spontaneous applause that erupted through the congregation. He motioned with his hands for the congregation to cease applauding, but they ignored him. The applause continued and the entire congregation rose to their feet. Steele was both flattered and embarrassed. He turned to look at his organist to see if he couldn't do something to help bring the congregation under control. The organist smiled and began a fanfare on the organ leading into the Doxology. The congregation sang loudly. When they were finished, there was even more applause.

"Thank you. Randi and I thank you for calling us to remain with you as your Rectory Family. I know that many of you are wondering just what went into our decision process. I want to share our thinking with you this morning. The opportunity that we were offered in Texas is one that most any priest would find desirable. The parish is in a rapidly growing section of San Antonio. It has a bright—no, it has a brilliant future. Their next Rector will be given the opportunity to not only build a new worship center, but fellowship and administrative buildings. It will be an exciting time for that Rector and for the people in that parish. Building a new church is an awesome responsibility and a wonderful opportunity."

Steele paused to look out at the congregation. "So you're asking yourselves, why would we not seize on that call and leave First Church behind us? The answer quite simply is because First Church does not need a new building. First Church has all the stained glass, organ pipes, brass, and wood paneling that she needs. One of the reasons I've chosen to stay here is precisely because we don't need any more of those things. The resources of First Church can best be directed to fulfill the words of Jesus that were read to you a few minutes ago in the Gospel. 'For as much as you have done it unto one of the least of these my children, you have done it unto me.'

There is a part of me that envies the next Rector of that parish in Texas. But the last few weeks have forced me to take a hard look at the kind of ministry I want to exercise. I came to understand that as beautiful as stained glass, organ pipes, and gothic spires can be, God has not placed a passion for these things in my heart. My heart is for the poor, the sick, the hungry, and the homeless. I have chosen to stay at First Church, first, because I've grown to love those of you who have allowed me to love you." There was an uncomfortable chuckle in the congregation.

"I'm committed to loving those of you who have not been able to receive me with the same charity." That sentence brought no chuckles. It was met with a silence and some knowing looks in the congregation. "Beyond my commitment to be the pastor to all the people in this parish, I'm committed to building on the ministry to the poor and needy in our community that we have already started. We've made a good start, but it's only a start. The words of Jesus are being realized every day in our Soup Kitchen, our Medical Clinic, and in our shelter for homeless men living with HIV and AIDS. These are only a start. There's so much more that we need to do."

Steele could see that he had everyone's attention, but there were a few folks that had decided that reading the bulletin or thumbing through the Prayer Book was a better use of their time. "It must be understood that these are not my pet projects or the fruits of a liberal, bleeding heart. These ministries incarnate the heart of our Lord. When we do these things for the least of his children, we do them unto him." Steele spotted Bud in the congregation. He was sitting with Almeda. "Just this past week a young man came to my office in need of help. His need was not unique to him. My preliminary research has helped me realize that there are other young men and women just like him sleeping under bridges and in cardboard boxes right here in Falls City. These young people are little more than children, but they are now homeless. Christian people cannot sleep carefree in their own beds when there are children not a stone's throw from this church that have no bed in which to sleep."

Steele surveyed the congregation. He once again had everyone's attention. "Last year, Randi and I were in San Francisco. One day we were approached by a homeless woman. She could not have been more than eighteen. She smelled of the streets. Her hands and face were covered with sores. She came up to me, 'Sir, can you please help me? I just need a few dollars to get something to eat.' I confess to you that I reached for my money clip to get out a few dollars in order to get rid of her. Then this young woman said something to me that cut right to my heart. She said, 'Sir, please look at me. Sir, will you please look at me?' I looked into her eyes and she continued. 'Sir, I used to be someone's little girl.' "

Steele stopped again and studied the faces sitting before him. Just as that girl's statement had touched his heart, it had touched the hearts of the congregation. "That homeless man that stands on the street corner with his cardboard sign used to be someone's little boy. More than that, every other one of them is a veteran of the armed services. They left their parent's homes as someone's little boy or girl to defend our nation against our enemies. They returned with heads filled with the horrors of war. They now walk the streets talking to the demons in their heads. They served our nation, now they have no place to go. No food to eat. No bed in which to sleep."

Steele paused once again. He looked out at the people he had chosen to continue to serve. "That woman pushing the shopping cart in the crosswalk in front of you used to be someone's little girl. The homeless disabled in their wheelchairs used to be someone's little girl or someone's little boy. And yes, those teens that I mentioned earlier used to be someone's little boy or someone's little girl, but through no fault of their own, they are now homeless.

First Church has enough stained glass, brass and organ pipes. We need no more. So what are we going to do with God's money?" Steele leaned forward on the pulpit and smiled. "I'm talking about God's money that's in all of our pockets, checkbooks, and safe deposit boxes." That comment was met with a chuckle. "I've chosen to remain as your Rector in order to help you spend some of God's money on those who have none of their own.

And they asked, 'when did we see you hungry, Lord? When did we see you thirsty or with no place to sleep? And Jesus answered, when you've done it unto one of the least of these, you have done it unto me.' "

Steele then turned and walked down the pulpit steps to his seat in the sanctuary. There was complete silence in the church. Horace Drummond asked the congregation to stand and affirm their faith in the words of the Nicene Creed. Steele stood as well. Then he noticed a shadow at the Sacristy door. It was Mrs. Gordon Smythe. Mrs. Smythe had been President of the Altar Guild for as long as anyone could remember. There was no heir apparent and no one dared challenge her for the position. She was whispering to the Verger. The Verger hastened up to Steele. He whispered in his ear. "The Altar Guild says that your wife just called on the Sacristy telephone. She is on her way to the hospital. She says that it's time. The baby is coming. She said for you to meet her at the hospital. She's already there."

CHAPTER 10

Robert Hayes was Bishop Rufus Petersen's best friend. If truth be told, he was his only friend. For some reason known only to the mystical forces, Bob Hayes loved Rufus Petersen. He was loyal to him to a fault. He had served as his legal advisor from the day Rufus was ordained a Bishop. There was probably no one on earth that knew the dark side of Rufus better. He had covered for his mismanagement of his Episcopal office and his ruthless use of power. Some of the things that he had done to the clergy in his care had given the Chancellor reason to pause. But out of love and loyalty for Rufus he covered for him.

He really didn't understand why Rufus did some of the things that he'd done. Some of his acts against his clergy had been downright cruel. He never hesitated using one of his infamous temper tantrums to control clergy. The Bishop had used rumor, innuendo, outright false accusation. He would even put his accusations in print and mail the letters to congregational leaders. He would do whatever was required to intimidate a priest he perceived as a threat. The accused priests were at his mercy. He knew that a Bishop's word would always carry more weight than that of a priest under suspicion. That Rufus got jealous of his own clergy's success could not be hidden from the Chancellor. Robert Hayes didn't understand it. After all, Rufus was the Bishop. He had maneuvered himself into what most lay people considered to be the top position in the Church. It seemed like that would be enough, but Rufus was in competition with everyone in his life. The one person he did not compete with was his good friend, Bob Hayes.

Rufus Petersen was sitting in the wingback chair next to the window in his master bedroom. He had the Sunday newspaper spread before him. He was still dressed in his purple pajamas and purple silk robe. When he was elected as Bishop of the Diocese of Savannah he re-decorated the master bedroom in his house the color worn by most bishops in the Episcopal Church—purple. He even had a headboard made out of woven cloth. The color, of course, was purple. His live-in servant announced the arrival of the Chancellor. "Misturh Hayes is here, Bishop. Kin I get you all anything to drink?"

Rufus looked up from his paper. "Bob, it's so good to see you. Thanks for coming. Can I get Clarence to bring you something?"

"It's good to see you, too, Rufus. I could use a cup of coffee."

"Yes, surh. Right away, surh. I'sa be right back. I'sa bring you some more that *erble* tea, Bishop."

"Rufus, you look really good. You look relaxed. And just look at you, you've lost so much weight"

"It's that damn doctor. My heart attacks didn't kill me so he's doing what he can to finish the job. He's got me going to the health center most every day to walk and exercise. He's even got me doing yoga."

The two men chuckled. "Well, whatever he has you doing it seems to be working. You look fantastic."

"Bob, do you have any idea what I'd give for shot of bourbon and big piece of prime rib?"

The Chancellor sat down in the wing chair opposite that of his beloved friend. "I'll bet if you keep doing just what you're doing we'll be able to celebrate before long with a glass of red wine and a small piece of red meat."

Rufus chuckled. "Oh, for the good ol' days of heavy drinking, overeating, and a twenty dollar cigar."

"Those days are gone, Rufus. But I'm just so thankful that you're getting well. I can forego all of that just for some good conversation and a piece of broiled fish."

Clarence entered with a silver tray with a silver pitcher of coffee on it. There was a smaller silver pitcher of cream and a silver bowl with sugar in it. "Does ya' want me to pour it for ya', Misturh Hayes?"

"No, just put it here on the table. I'll pour it myself."

"Here's yor tea, Bishop. You all want anything else?"

"No, thanks, Clarence." Rufus waved for him to leave the two men alone. When Bob had poured himself a cup of coffee, Rufus smiled gently at his friend. "Were you able to locate him?"

Bob Hayes nodded. "It took some doing, but we found him. We started up in Atlanta. That's where he moved first. When he left Centerville he was selling Fords at a dealership up there."

"Yes, I remember." Rufus was silent. "Bob, I now know that what we allowed those people to do to that man and his family was so wrong. I could have stopped them."

"Oh, I don't know, Rufus. He'd offended all the wrong people in that parish. They were out to get him and they weren't going to stop until they'd destroyed him."

Rufus grimaced, "Since I asked you to locate him, I haven't been able to get the scene in my office that day out of my mind. Do you remember?"

The Chancellor nodded. "I remember. That group down there in Centerville hired a couple of women to accuse him of misconduct. He denied it. You and I both knew that he hadn't done anything. His wife pleaded with us to help him. We even got letters from members of the congregation to intercede."

"The thing I can't get out of my mind is him down on his knees in my office begging me not to take his priesthood away from him." Rufus shivered. "I don't know what I was thinking. I could've helped him, but I just didn't want to go up against the powerbrokers in that parish."

"I know. As you've said so many times, we can always get another priest. Another parish is a little harder to come by."

"So you found him."

"He's actually done quite well for himself. He's now a stockbroker at a big firm in Atlanta."

"A stockbroker?"

"Yeah, and from what I could see, he's quite successful. He was wearing a tailored suit that had to cost a couple of thousand dollars. He had a family picture on his desk that was taken in front of his house in Atlanta. Rufus, it's a mansion."

"So you got to talk to him?"

"He wasn't particularly pleased to see me, so I had to get right to the point."

"Did you tell him that I wanted to reinstate his priesthood?"

Bob Hayes shook his head grimly. "That part didn't go so well. I'm afraid he's really angry with us. He gave me some very choice words to pass on to you. I guess the kindest way that I can put it to you is…well, he told me to tell you to take your priesthood and put in an obscene part of your anatomy."

Rufus was silent. He tried to speak, but had to clear his throat. "Did you tell him that I wanted to meet with him? Did you tell him I want to apologize? I want to ask him to forgive me?"

Bob looked into his friend's eyes. He saw something there that he'd never seen before. He saw genuine contrition. Rufus Petersen really did want to make amends with a priest he'd allowed some antagonists to destroy. "Rufus, my friend, that's just not going to happen. The only thing that man wants for you is that you will take a long trip to a very warm climate. He wants you to stay there for eternity."

A tear dropped down the cheek of the Bishop of Savannah. He wiped it away with the back of his hand. "Maybe if I were to go see him myself?"

"Rufus, I wouldn't recommend that. That man is not going to forgive you. The only thing he wants from you is to be left alone. I think you just need to let him go."

Rufus sat quietly. Then he reached into the drawer in the table beside his chair. "Here's a list of other priests that I feel like I've failed. I'd like for you to try to arrange a meeting with each of them."

The Chancellor studied the list for a few minutes. He shook his head and looked back at the Bishop. "My friend, I know that your intentions are pure, but I just don't think any of these men are going to want to hear anything you have to say."

"That may be so, but I've just got to try."

"Have you thought about Steele Austin? Did he respond to the letter you wrote him before you got sick?"

"I got a prayer card from him. He wrote a note saying that I was in his prayers for a complete recovery, but he didn't say anything about my letter. I don't guess I blame him. Maybe, just maybe that's a priest that will listen to me."

"Since he's still under your authority, he has to listen to you."

Rufus stared out the window. The two men sat in silence. "Just as soon as the doctor gives me the go-ahead, I want to drive down to Falls City to meet with him. Will you go with me?"

Robert Hayes nodded. "I'll do whatever you need me to do, Rufus. I always have and I guess I always will."

CHAPTER 11

Steele hurried into the Sacristy. Mrs. Gordon Smythe was waiting on him. "Just give me your vestments. I'll take care of them. You need to get to the hospital as fast as you can. Go out the Sacristy door. Chief Sparks is waiting on you. He'll drive you to the hospital. I told him that Randi was already there. He said he can get you there the quickest."

Steele uttered, "Thanks you, thank you so much." He was shaking like a leaf.

"Clearly, you're in no shape to drive. I'm glad that I asked the Chief to get you there."

"I'm just so excited and nervous."

"Hurry on now. Tell Randi that we're all pulling for her."

When Steele opened the Sacristy door, he saw that Chief Sparks was leaning against his car. He was chewing on his signature cigar. "It's too soon to be smoking a cigar," Steele smiled.

"Come on, Parson. You know I never smoke these things. They'll kill you."

"Thanks for volunteering to drive me."

"Volunteer, hell, Mrs. Smythe commandeered both me and this city vehicle. She told me that if I don't get you to the hospital before your baby is born, I'll have to answer to her. Now I don't know about you, but I don't want to have to answer to any of those ladies on that Altar Guild. You and I both know that they're *cotton on iron.*"

Steele opened the door and quickly slid into the front seat. "You going to use your siren and lights?"

The Chief chuckled. "I don't think that'll be necessary. All the officers know my car. There shouldn't be any problem."

"The Chief pulled into the hospital circle. Steele jumped out of the car. "Thanks so much. I owe you one."

"You don't owe me a thing, Padre. Just give Randi a big hug for me."

Steele waved and ran into the hospital. He took the elevator to the third floor nurses station. "I'm Steele Austin. My wife Randi is here."

The nurse looked up from her chart. "Oh yes, Father, you really need to hurry. I'm afraid things are moving quite fast. The doctor has already taken your wife into the delivery room. You know the drill. Go get your mask and gown on. Scrub your hands and then I'll take you to her."

Steele remembered where to find the gowns and masks from the prenatal classes that Randi and he had taken. His hands were shaking as he fumbled to put first the robe on, then the coverings over his shoes, a surgical cap and mask. Just outside the dressing area there was a sink where he could scrub his hands. Just as he was drying them the nurse entered. "Come on, your baby is about to be born and you're going to miss it. Let's go!"

The nurse led Steele down a short hallway and through a swinging metal door. Randi was sitting up on a bed. A nurse was propping her up with pillow. Randi was breathing deeply as she had rehearsed in the classes. Steele hurried to her side. Her voice was hoarse, "Oh thank God, I was afraid you weren't going to make it."

"I'm sorry, Honey. I got here as fast as I could."

"Well, you're here now, Daddy. This baby wants to get a look at your face." The doctor spoke through her mask. "You ready, Randi?"

"Randi nodded. She squeezed Steele's hand. "Ohhhh…."

"Good, good…now take a couple of deep breaths," the doctor instructed. Randi did as she was told. After just a minute the doctor shouted, "now, Randi, now. Push! Push!"

Randi groaned and then the room was filled with the sounds of a new life. Randi collapsed back on the pillow. "It's a girl!" the doctor announced. She's a beautiful baby girl."

Steele wiped the sweat from his wife's face with a cool cloth. She grabbed his hand, "Steele, check. Remember, you were going to check first thing."

The doctor held the baby up so that they could see her. Steele quickly did an inventory of his new daughter. He broke out in a big smile. "Ten fingers, ten toes, everything is where it's supposed to be."

Randi uttered, "Thank you, God. Thank you."

The doctor asked, "Steele, do you want to cut the cord?"

Steele nodded.

"Here." The nurse pointed to a place on the cord between two clamps. "Here."

When the cord was cut, the nurse wrapped the baby in a blanket and handed her to Steele. "Here's your daughter."

The doctor looked at Steele and the baby. "Have you ever seen so much black hair? She looks just like you, Father." Then the doctor glanced over at the nurse. "Well, at least we know who the daddy is. I wonder who the mother is?"

"That's not funny," Randi hissed.

Steele carried his new daughter to his wife's side. He gently laid her in Randi's arms. "You, little girl, are the luckiest little girl in the world. This is your mommy. She is the best mommy any little girl could ever hope to have."

Randi leaned up on her side so she could get a closer look at her baby. "My gosh, Steele, the doctor is right. She looks just like you. Look at all this black hair."

The nurse came to the bedside. "We really need to go ahead and get her cleaned up. After you get to your room, I'll bring her to you."

Randi kissed her new daughter on her forehead. Steele leaned over and did the same. Then he kissed his wife.

"Have you decided on a name?" The nurse asked.

Steele nodded. "Yes, we have. Randi, I want you to be the first to say her name to her."

Randi smiled at her husband. "Steele, I've been thinking about the name we chose. If it's all right with you I'd like to give her another name."

Steele was surprised. "Well…if you're sure. I mean, we talked about it so much. I thought that we'd decided."

"I know, but I don't think you'll be disappointed." She took Steele's hand. "Honey, I know that your grandmother meant so much to you. You've said that if it weren't for her you probably wouldn't even be a committed Christian and you certainly wouldn't be a priest."

Steele nodded.

Randi smiled at him again and squeezed his hand all the tighter. "Steele, I want to name our baby after your grandmother. Steele, I want to name her Amanda Ellen."

Tears streamed down Steele's cheeks. He leaned over and kissed his wife on the lips. "I love you so much. I love you for giving me our beautiful daughter. Thank you, Randi. Thank you for loving me. Thank you for naming our daughter after my little grandmother. I just know that there are big smiles in heaven right now."

The nurse once again reached to take the baby from Randi's arms. Steele stopped her. "I need to do one more thing." He leaned over and made the sign of the cross on his daughter's forehead. "Amanda Ellen, I bless you. Welcome to this world and to our family."

CHAPTER 12

Ned Boone, Elmer, and Judith Idle were huddled over their Bloody Marys at a table at the Falls City Country Club. They had agreed to meet there for Sunday Brunch after church. The room was filled with some of Falls City's finest citizens. The Dexters were at an adjoining table. Ned nodded in their direction in order to make sure that the Idles were aware of their presence. He also motioned with his eyes toward the Henry Mudds when they entered. They had already gone to the buffet tables. The two little Mudd girls were following a couple of the club waiters that were carrying their plates for them. They were seated at a table on the far side of the dining room. There were still other couples and families from First Church seated about the dining room.

Ned spoke in a hushed voice. "What do you think is going on with Henry Mudd?"

Judith Idle turned to look at them. "Why? What on earth do you mean, Ned?"

He puckered his mouth. "I don't know. It's just that things don't seem right with him. He's lost a lot of weight. He just seems to be so stressed, no, he just looks so unhappy."

Elmer nodded. "I've noticed the same thing about him. But Virginia, on the other hand, seems to be picking up all the weight that Henry is losing. She's really chunking up."

Judith chimed in. "I have seen Henry down at the parish house quite a bit recently. I even saw him hugging the Rector one day in the hallway outside Steele's office."

Ned grimaced. "I was afraid of that. I feared that he'd joined the Steele Austin fan club. I tell you, Austin is as slick as they come. I think he could con the Angel Gabriel."

Elmer took a long gulp of his Bloody Mary. He turned and motioned for the waiter to bring another round to the table. "I know that you're right. He's a real pro, but I never thought he'd be able to pull the wool over Henry Mudd's eyes."

"Well, that means that Mudd is not going to help us."

They all sat in silence as the waiter brought their drinks and put them on the table in front of each of them. When the waiter had moved out of earshot, Judith leaned forward. "What about the Bishop?"

Ned shook his head. "Who knows if he'll even be going back to his office? From what I can gather, he's in pretty bad shape. I don't think he'll be of any use to us."

Elmer had already downed his second drink and was motioning for the waiter to bring him a third one. "Well, you both heard the sermon this morning."

"And what a sorry excuse for a sermon it was." Ned spewed. "That priest is hell bent on pursuing his bleeding heart ministry to every lazy deadbeat he can find. It's like he runs around town looking for problems. Then he wants to throw our hard earned money at them."

Elmer took the drink from the silver tray that the waiter was holding. He then waved the waiter away with his other hand. "I'll be damned if we can stand back and just let him squander the precious treasury of First Church. I don't want my tithe going to a bunch of deadbeats who are just too lazy to work."

Judith put her hand on her husband's arm. "Now, now Elmer, there's no reason to use profanity. Jesus would not be pleased."

Elmer smiled at his wife. "I know that He wouldn't. I apologize to you and to you, Ned. I'll ask Jesus to forgive me when we do our devotions together this evening."

Judith beamed. "Isn't my husband a wonderful man, Ned?"

"Yes, Judith. I know that he is. That's why I'm doing everything in my power to see that he gets elected the next Senior Warden at First Church." He glanced over at Howard Dexter, who was sitting at the next table. He leaned in toward the center of the table and the Idles did the same. He whispered, "Our current Senior Warden has been a real disappointment. I thought sure he would be able to get rid of this recalcitrant priest, but no such luck. I'm not so sure Dexter over there hasn't become president of Steele Austin's fan club."

Elmer and Judith nodded. Then Elmer whispered, "I promise you this. If I do become the Senior Warden, I'm going to be riding Steele Austin like one of those bull riders in an Oklahoma rodeo. Every time he turns around he's going to find me watching him. I'll question his every move and demand an explanation for his every breath. I will make his life miserable." Elmer punched the air with his finger to emphasize his threat.

Ned smiled. "That's exactly what's needed. He's going to wish that he'd seized on that opportunity to move to Texas. Our only hope is to wear him down to the point that he'll throw in the towel."

"Don't you think that we can investigate him further?" Judith Idle questioned. "I mean, I'm still convinced that he framed our Business Manager. Ted Holmes was innocent. Steele Austin set him up in order to cover his own crimes. I tell you, the wrong man is in prison."

Elmer and Ned nodded. Then Ned whispered again, "I called the prosecutor and told them as much, but I got nowhere."

"Then let's just wear him down." Judith agreed. "We have to do it before he destroys our church."

Elmer patted his wife's hand. "I agree that he's so slick we'll never be able to catch him in his tricks. If only I could just wipe that cocky smile off his face..." Elmer paused. He gritted his front teeth as his eyes bulged. His face turned dark red. "I promise you, I'll put the pressure on him and I'll keep it on him. He'll grow to hate the sound of my voice. But it won't do him any good. I'll put his every word under the microscope. I'm going to put so much pressure on him that he'll not be able to think straight." Elmer sat back in his chair and took another large swallow of his drink. "He'll resign, I tell you. It'll be the only way he can get any relief. He won't be able to get out of town fast enough. He'll be so happy to leave that he'll think that the prettiest thing he's ever seen in his life is the sight of First Church in his rear view mirror."

All sat in silence for a few minutes. Then Ned smiled, "there's one more thing I need to share with you."

"Oh?" Elmer and Judith blurted at the same time.

Once again Ned leaned into the center of the table and the Idles followed suit. He whispered, "I think we need to continue to investigate, but we need to shift the focus of our investigation."

Judith's eyes grew large. "Are you thinking what I'm thinking, Ned?"

Ned nodded, "If you mean the wife, then yes, we're thinking the same thing."

Judith smirked. "I've not liked her from the day they arrived. She's just a bit too sweet to suit me. I really don't think anyone can be that nice."

"Unless you have something to hide," Ned grunted.

Elmer swallowed the last of his third drink. "Things are really beginning to fall in place. Steele has been running a diversion on us. He's kept the focus on himself so we wouldn't investigate his wife. I tell you, that man could teach lessons to the mafia bosses."

"Do you suspect anything in particular, Ned?" Judith was beaming with anticipation.

Ned returned her smile. "Just stay tuned. I have some suspicions. If they prove to be true, Steele Austin will be someone else's problem. First Church will be saved."

Judith lifted both of her hands in front of her chest with her palms upward toward the heavens, "Oh, thank you, Jesus. Bless you, Ned. God bless you."

Elmer smiled. "Perhaps we should go to the buffet and get our plates, but before we do, let's ask Judith to lead us in prayer."

Judith could not hide her own satisfaction as she watched the two men bow their heads. Judith than prayed in a voice loud enough for all those at the surrounding tables to hear, "Lord Jesus, I'm so thankful for my wonderful husband. You've so blessed my life by giving me this holy man to be my companion. I'm also thankful for your faithful servant, Ned. He so loves you and so loves our church. I just lift up both of these me to you. Bless them, Jesus. Continue to bless them for they are a blessing. My heart is so filled with gratitude for these two righteous men. Lord, you know that their hearts are pure and filled with a hunger to do your will. Jesus, you love us so much and you continue to show us that love in these two good men. Thank you, Jesus. Thank you. Now continue to bless us and the food we are to receive."

The two men responded with a lusty, "Amen."

CHAPTER 13

"Congratulations, Daddy!" Henry Mudd was standing at the door to Steele's office. "You getting any sleep?"

"Well, I can imagine that you still have some memory of early morning feedings."

"Are Randi and the baby both doing well?"

"Both are in good shape. Randi is worrying about getting into her skinny clothes, so I guess that's a good sign."

Henry Mudd walked into Steele's office for his weekly conference. The first person that Henry had told about his wife's adultery was Steele Austin. He had taken him into his confidence and exposed his hurt and pain to Steele. Since that first night, they had met weekly for spiritual nurture and guidance. "Steele, I'm really glad that you're going to stay with us at First Church."

Steele smiled and shook Henry's hand. "Thanks Henry, Randi and I are really happy about our decision as well." He motioned for Henry to take a seat on the sofa. Steele resumed his usual position in a wingback chair opposite the couch. Steele's mind flashed back to the evolution of his relationship with Henry. Henry used to literally spit his words at Steele. He refused to call him *Father* and often would address him as *Padre*. But that was usually done with a mocking tone in his voice. Henry had worked diligently to remove Steele from First Church. Now, he was allowing Steele to be his pastor and his friend. He addressed him by his name, *Steele*. He did so with a genuine affection in his voice.

"I'm not sure I would have made the same decision that you did, Steele. I'm the first to admit my role in it all, but this place has not treated you and your little family with much charity."

Steele smiled and nodded, "I hope all of that is behind us."

Henry sat back on the couch and crossed his legs. "Maybe, but I know that you're no fool. You realize there's still a group here intent on doing you in."

"Their numbers are pretty small now. I think most everyone sees what they've been trying to do."

"Steele, I'm here to help you in any way that I can, but don't underestimate them. I know these people. They'll stop at nothing. They'll fabricate whatever they have to fabricate and then manufacture evidence to support their accusations."

"Well, let's just hope that you and I don't have to battle them by ourselves. I think I have the overwhelming support of the parish."

Henry nodded, "You do. But Steele, they may only represent one or two percent of the parish but they believe themselves to be the right two percent. Their desires overrule the majority. They think that they're entitled to get their way."

Steele had been watching Henry's body language since his arrival. He seemed unusually nervous, even agitated. He was having a difficult time finding a comfortable position on the couch. "You didn't come in here to talk to me about the antagonists at First Church. Henry, something else is bothering you. Talk to me."

Henry's face turned bright red. An uncomfortable laugh shook his body. He glanced at Steele and then quickly looked out the window of Steele's office. "I think I need to make a confession."

Steele leaned forward toward Henry. "Do you want to tell me something in confidence or do you want to make a formal confession?"

Henry met Steele's eyes. "Can't we just talk? I mean…I really need to get something off my chest."

"Okay, but whatever you tell me will remain in this office. We'll consider it *under the seal.*"

Henry nodded and then blushed again. "Steele, while I was in Las Vegas last week I did something I've never done in my life." Henry's voice broke and a tear dropped down his cheek.

Steele handed him a tissue from the box on the side table next to his chair. "Go on, Henry. You know that you're in a safe place."

Henry's voice continued to hold back the sobs as he uttered his confession to Steele. "I hired a prostitute."

"And now you feel guilty?"

Henry shook his head. "Yes and no. Nothing happened. I mean, we both got undressed and she did try to arouse me, but nothing happened. I mean, I wanted to….." His voice drifted off and once again he stared out the window. "You know, maybe I really didn't want to." Henry smiled as he looked back at Steele, "She was absolutely beautiful. She may have been one of the most beautiful women I've ever seen in my life, but I just couldn't."

Steele nodded.

Henry leaned forward, "Hell, Steele, I've only been with one woman in my entire life. I guess that makes me some kind of nerd or something. When Virginia and I married I was a virgin. I've never wanted to be with any other woman but her."

"So why do you think you hired the prostitute?"

Another tear dropped down Henry's cheek. His eyes began to fill. His voice broke again as he expressed his pain, "Since I found out...you know, I've just been so damn lonely. I just want to feel a woman want me. I need to hold a woman and feel her needing me to hold her. I want to feel her naked body in my arms. And Steele, at this point I really didn't care whether she is a prostitute or a pick-up in a bar."

"Were you able to do any of those things with...?"

Henry interrupted, "Please, don't call her a prostitute. I don't know whether it was her real name or not." Henry forced a chuckle. "She told me her name was Gigi. I don't suppose that was her real name."

Steele joined Henry with a chuckle of his own, "You think?"

Henry sat back on the couch. He had regained his composure. "It was really nice. I loved the feel of holding her. It felt so good. I think she really wanted to be with me. I don't think it was just about the money. I mean, maybe it's wishful thinking on my part, but I felt like she really wanted to be with me." Henry leaned forward and looked down at the floor. "Steele, I'm ashamed to tell you just how really good it felt to be with her. I enjoyed talking to her. She really listened to me. It felt so nice to have this beautiful young woman try to please me."

"Henry, my friend, you're still in a lot of pain. It only makes sense that you'd feel isolated and lonely. Your ego has taken a real bruising. It only makes sense that you want to feel needed in every way. Your manhood was attacked and now you feel the need to repair it."

"It really wasn't about sex, Steele." Henry exhaled deeply as he sat back on the couch. "I know that it sounds like such a cliché, but honest to God, that wasn't it. I'm just so damn lonely." Once again, tears welled up in his eyes. "I just want someone to love me. And even though I was paying for it, for a couple of hours I really enjoyed talking to this woman. She really understood me. Did I tell you that she's studying to be a counselor?"

Steele smiled, "Henry, it sounds like she was just what the doctor ordered."

"Are you telling me that it's okay for me to go to hookers?"

Steele chuckled. "Now Henry, you're smarter than that. I'm just telling you that it was rather fortuitous that the hooker you called was also studying to be a counselor."

"I guess it was too much to hope that you'd give me your blessing to keep an escort service on my speed dial."

Steele smiled broadly at Henry and he smiled back. "Like I said, you're a lot smarter than that."

"What am I going to do?" Henry held his hands out toward Steele as though pleading for an answer. "What am I going to do for companionship? I'm a man. I need a woman to let me know that she desires me more than any other man in her life. I want to be the man she's thinking about when she closes her eyes. Damn it, I have to believe that I'm not just the man in her life. I'm her only man."

Once again Steele nodded his understanding.

Henry slowly shook his head. A look of disgust crossed his face. "Virginia has already destroyed her hope of doing that for me. She's already shown me that I wasn't number one in her life. She lied to me so she could run off and be with someone else. He was her number one. He was more important to her than I was or our marriage. She'll never be able to make me feel special again."

"Henry, do you remember me telling you what you need to do if you decided to remain with her? If you don't work on forgiving her and rebuilding your marriage, you've doomed yourself to a lifetime of loneliness?"

Henry looked out the window and sat in silence. "I remember."

"I fear that you already know the answer to your own question."

A look of indignation crossed Henry's face. "We've been through all that, Steele. My answer is the same. How can I ever trust that woman to love me and make me first in her life? Just look at how far she was willing to go in order to give herself to another man."

"It begins with forgiveness. Virginia has asked you to forgive her."

"Spoken like the priest that you are, but I'm not so sure she's sorry she did it. I think she's just sorry she got caught."

The look of indignation on Henry's face grew even more severe. He looked first at Steele and then out of the window. He stood and began to pace around Steele's office. Steele watched him. Henry went over to Steele's office window and stood with his back to Steele. It then became apparent to him that Henry was crying. Steele stood and walked over to the end of his desk where Henry was standing. He sat down on the edge of his desk. He reached for a tissue in the box on his desk and handed it to Henry. Henry took a tissue and wiped his eyes. "Henry, is there something you're not telling me?"

Henry continued to stare out the window. "Steele, she's pregnant. My wife is pregnant with that Frenchman's baby."

A sick feeling struck Steele in the pit of his stomach like a bolt of lightning. He felt his own knees grow weak. He was soaking up Henry's pain. He was so glad that he was sitting on top of his desk. "Henry, I had no idea."

"I just found out this morning. I'd suspected it, but as of this morning I'm positive."

"Are you sure that the baby isn't yours?"

"I've had a vasectomy. After our second daughter was born, I had myself fixed. We'd always agreed on two children and no more. The baby is not mine."

Henry turned and glared at Steele. "Now, what kind of priestly advice would you like to give me? Do you still want to preach your forgiveness sermon for me?"

Steele was at a loss for words. He really didn't have any answers for Henry. "I'm so sorry. I honestly don't know what to say to you. I've never had a situation like yours presented to me before."

Henry nodded and walked back to the sofa. He seated himself, leaned forward and placed his face in his hands. Great sobs poured out of him. Steele sat next to Henry on the couch and put his hand on his shoulder. "Henry, I really am sorry. I just wish I had a magic wand or some great words of wisdom to comfort you with, but this has really caught me off guard."

After a few minutes Henry wiped his face with a fresh tissue and sat back on the couch. Steele returned to his seat. The two men sat in silence.

Steele desperately searched his mind for some words to share with Henry, but his search was in vain. "What is she going to do about the baby?"

"You mean her bastard?"

Steele did not respond.

"Frankly, I don't care what she does. The one thing she won't be doing is bringing that frog's child into my house for me to raise. She's humiliated me beyond words. I'll not let her add insult to my injury."

"The two of you have a really difficult decision to make."

"No sir!" Henry shouted. "She has a decision to make. I don't want to know anything about what she decides. I've made it very clear to her what she cannot do. Beyond that, I honestly don't care."

Once again a dark silence entered the room. Steele was at a complete loss for words. Henry stared out the window. After a long pause, Steele broke the silence. "Do you want me to pray with you, Henry?"

Henry stood and started walking to the door. "I'd rather you not. I'm not too happy with God right now. I really don't have anything to say to Him."

Steele followed Henry to the door. He had never felt so inadequate in a pastoral situation in his life. "Henry, I just wish I could help you. I'm disappointed in myself that I can't offer some words of comfort or wisdom."

Henry turned and smiled back at Steele. "You're a good man, Steele Austin. I really hate burdening you with my problems."

"Henry I just wish I could do more."

"You're doing all that can be expected of any priest, Steele. Thanks for being here for me. Thanks for listening and thanks for understanding." Henry turned again to open the door and then turned back to look at Steele. "And what I've told you today?"

Steele patted Henry on his back. "It stays here with me, Henry. It will go with me to my grave. No other living person will ever learn from me what you shared with me today."

Henry nodded and opened the door. "I'm really glad that you're going to stay with us at First Church."

"Thanks, Henry. Call me if you need me." Steele stood in the hallway outside his office and watched Henry pass through the doors and out of the building. He couldn't get beyond the feeling that there was something more he could have said to him, but his mind was a complete blank. Then he remembered a piece of wisdom that his little grandmother had passed on to him. Sometimes there simply are no easy answers. There are just a lot of bad choices.

CHAPTER 14

Randi had finished nursing Amanda. It was her mid-morning feeding. The baby was now sleeping soundly. She carried her to her crib and put her on her stomach. The new mom was exhausted. Steele had volunteered to do the early morning feedings if Randi would use a breast pump, but she just couldn't bring herself to do that just yet. She cherished the time she had with her new daughter. Maybe later on when she was a little older she would take him up on his offer, but for now she wanted that time all to herself. Besides, she could always nap when Amanda was sleeping. Steele's work didn't allow him that luxury. She stretched out on the bed and closed her eyes. Sleep was just rolling over her when the doorbell rang. She sat up and looked out her bedroom window. She recognized the car in the front driveway. It belonged to Martha Dexter. The doorbell rang again.

Randi slid her feet into her slippers and took a quick glance in the dresser mirror. The doorbell rang yet one more time. She knew that Martha would not give up. She would continue to ring the bell until it woke up Amanda or it was answered. She quickly applied some lipstick and hurried down the stairs to the front door. She faked a smile and opened the door. To her surprise, there stood both Mrs. Gordon Smythe and Martha Dexter. "Good Morning, ladies."

"Good Morning, Randi." Mrs. Smythe chirped. "We do hope that we haven't caught you at a bad time. I told Martha that we should have telephoned before coming over, but she insisted that the ringing of the phone might waken the baby."

Randi realized that the women were carrying a gift-wrapped package. "Oh, you shouldn't have brought us another gift. You both have already been far too generous." She opened the door further and motioned for the women to enter. "Let's go into the living room. May I offer you some coffee or tea?"

"We don't want to be any trouble." The women cooed in unison.

"Oh, it's not a problem. I believe there's still some coffee in the kitchen. Would that be acceptable?"

"That would be very nice." Mrs. Smythe smiled.

Randi turned to walk toward the kitchen when she realized that the two women were following her. She turned to look at them. "Oh, I'll bring it to you in the living room."

Martha Dexter kept walking toward her with Mrs. Smythe on her trail. Martha insisted, "Nonsense, we'll just have coffee with you in the kitchen. I told you we didn't want to be any trouble."

Randi realized that she was not going to dissuade these two very strong-willed women. "But ladies, I've not even had time to remove the breakfast dishes from the table."

"Then we'll just help you with that." Martha hastened her pace behind Randi. When they arrived in the kitchen the two women immediately began clearing the table and putting the dishes in the dishwasher. Randi reached in the cupboard for some coffee cups and saucers. "I'm afraid the only sweets that I have to offer you are some of Travis's Oreo Cookies."

"Oh, I love Oreo Cookies." Martha Dexter smiled.

Randi poured the coffee into the cups and placed them in front of the women who were now seated at the table. She put a plate of Oreo Cookies in the middle of the table. Martha Dexter immediately reached for two of them. After just a couple of bites she had chocolate crumbs and white frosting on her lips. She spewed the crumbs in her mouth onto the table as she spoke, "Mary Alice, give her the present."

Mary Alice Smythe put her hand to her heart. "Oh, I almost forgot. Randi, I hope you'll like it."

Randi took the package and began opening it. "You really shouldn't have done this. Amanda will never be able to wear all the clothes that this parish has given her."

The two women giggled. "This present is not for Amanda, it's for you."

A confused look crossed Randi's face as she continued to open the package. She saw Martha Dexter wink at Mrs. Smythe. "Oh, my gosh…" Randi squealed. "What have the two of you done?"

"Well, we just might not be as square as you young people think we are." Randi lifted the white two piece bikini bathing suit out of the package. The three women laughed all the more.

"I don't know. Just what do you think some of the fine folks at First Church would think if they saw the Rector's wife wearing this at the next pool party?"

Martha Dexter reached for two more cookies and crammed the first one in her mouth. "Oh, who cares what they think. If I had a figure like yours, I'd wear it at every opportunity."

Randi placed her hand over her heart and faked surprise, "Why, Mrs. Dexter I just never thought you'd approve of such a thing." All three women were united in laughter yet one more time.

"I agree with Martha." Mary Alice Smythe smiled. "Just look at you. You just had a baby and you're already getting your cute little figure back. We want you to wear it and wear it with pride. If anyone gives you any grief, just tell them it was a gift from us."

Martha Dexter had now stuffed her fourth cookie in her mouth and her lips were covered all the more with dark chocolate crumbs. "May we get a peek at the baby?"

"Well, she's sleeping right now, but I guess it'll be okay. I'd just put her down." The three women followed Randi up the stairs to the nursery. Once inside, they whispered the anticipated oohs and aahs. "She is such a good mix of the two of you."

Randi smiled, "Oh, I don't know. Most everyone says she's the spitting image of her daddy."

"Nonsense," Mary Alice shook her head. "She's every bit as pretty as her mother. You just wait and see. She's going to be a real heart breaker."

Once they were back in the kitchen and seated at the table, Martha Dexter took the last two cookies from the plate. "Do you want me to get more cookies?" Randi smiled.

Mary Alice answered quickly, "No, I believe we've had plenty." She then shot a look at Martha Dexter, who continued to chew the last cookie. "We do have just a bit of business we'd like to conduct with you."

"Oh?"

"We really hope you don't mind, but we made the decision to help you find a house that would be suitable for the Rector of First Church to live in."

Randi wrinkled her brow. She was confused. "I don't understand."

Mary Alice reached into her purse and brought out three sheets of paper. Randi recognized them as real estate flyers for houses that were for sale. "Well, as you know, the Rector of First Church has a certain image to uphold. We need you to live in the right section of our city. We also need you to have a home that is suitable for parish entertainment, but at the same time it must not be too lavish."

Martha Dexter interrupted, "But it needs to be nicer than the manses that the Presbyterians or Methodists keep their preachers in. We won't have them upstage us on that one."

"Ladies, we've not even thought about looking for a house just yet. We may not do so for several weeks or even a few more months."

"There's no need." Mary Alice rebutted. "We've done all the hard work for you. I can't tell you the number of houses we've reviewed on your behalf, but that doesn't matter. We've decided that any one of these three would be acceptable to the parish."

Randi was on the verge of tears as she fought to maintain a smile and her composure. She glanced at each of the flyers. None of them were even close to any-thing that she and Steele had talked about. None of them were in neighborhoods with children. They were all in established neighborhoods with older residents. They'd wanted to be in a young neighborhood where there would be lots of children for Travis and Amanda to play with. All these were older homes. She and Steele had dreamed of a new home that they could either build from scratch or decorate themselves. Randi realized that Mrs. Smythe and Mrs. Dexter had been doing a running commentary on each house as she was looking at the flyers. "This one was particularly acceptable to the Altar Guild."

Randi shook her head in an effort to bring herself out of a daze of disbelief. "…The Altar Guild?"

"Why yes, Randi," Mary Alice patted her hand. "It's critical that the Altar Guild approve of the house that you and Steele are going to live in. After all, our Altar Guild is composed of women of refinement and good taste in this city. You're getting the benefit of all their counsel and wisdom."

Randi glanced over at Martha Dexter. The cookie crumbs and white frosting were still on her lips. Martha smiled at Randi and her front teeth were caked with dark cookie dough. The words *good taste and refinement* forced her to smile.

Mary Alice misinterpreted her smile. "We just knew you'd be pleased with our work. We'll go now and leave these flyers for you to show Misturh Austin. The name of the realtor we've selected for you to use is on one of the flyers. That's also the home that is the first choice of the Altar Guild."

The two women stood and started down the hallway toward the front door. They stopped at the entrance and looked around. Mary Alice sighed, "I do so hate to see you give up this Rectory. It's such a beautiful home. It's just been so perfectly situated for our parish events. Nevertheless, we understand that you young people want your own home. I just know that you'll find one of those that we selected for you acceptable."

Randi nodded. She wasn't sure just how much longer she would be able to fight back her tears. She forced a smile and the two ladies exited. She had no more than closed the door when she leaned back against it, slid to the floor, and let the disappointment pour out of her.

CHAPTER 15

Alicia Thompson had been Virginia Mudd's shield. She had helped cover up her affair with Jacque. She had provided her lake house to them for their weekly rendezvous. There were other occasions when she provided her with the cover story she needed to keep Henry off track. Then there were the dinner parties at her house in Falls City. Jacque would join her at Alicia's for their "girl's night out." There they would share a joint, some drinks, and dinner. Then Alicia would go outside or take a drive so that they could use her guest room for romance. Alicia was the only person that knew that Virginia was having an affair.

"I don't know what I'm going to do." Virginia sobbed.

"Henry knows that you're pregnant?"

Virginia nodded. "He's furious. I don't think he'll ever forgive me."

"Then divorce him." Alicia snorted.

"And go where?" Virginia's eyes were red and swollen with grief. "He'll take my girls from me. He'll make the videos and pictures he has of me public. I'll be designated as the town whore. I'll have no money, no home, and no friends. My reputation will be ruined. My children will disown me."

Alicia lit a cigarette and pulled the smoke deep into her lungs. She exhaled, "You told me you didn't think you loved him, so why stay with him? Go to a new town. Get a fresh start."

"Henry was good to me. I was just too self centered and needy to see it."

Alicia walked over to the refrigerator and brought back a bottle of white wine. She poured Virginia a glass and then poured herself one. "Boy, your story is really changing now. I thought he didn't meet your needs. I thought he was selfish with the money. Virginia, just what is your story?"

Virginia took a sip of the wine. "Alicia, I thought you were my friend. I didn't come here to have you throw my words back in my face."

Alicia took another drag from her cigarette. "I am your friend. I'm just confused as to how you got into this mess."

Virginia nodded. "I'm a fool. I'm a damn fool, Alicia. Now I've lost everything."

"What about Jacque? Have you talked to him?"

"I bought one of those prepaid telephone calling cards and called him while Henry was in Las Vegas. He's now up in Raleigh. He has an acting job in a dinner theatre."

"Well, does he still love you?"

"Oh, you know Jacque. Right now Henry has him terrified. He knows he'll never work again as a museum director. Henry and his cronies have made sure of that. But he's dirt poor. He was really cold and distant. He just told me that I needed to get on with my life."

"That doesn't sound like love."

"I don't think it ever was for him. I think I was just a plaything. He used me for sex. I don't think he really ever loved me. I was just a thrill."

Alicia opened another bottle of wine. She filled each of their glasses. "Did you tell him about the baby?"

Virginia took a big swallow of her wine and shook her head.

"Didn't you all use protection?"

Tears streamed down Virginia's face. "Yes, we were extremely careful. I told Jacque that we had to be. I told him that Henry had had a vasectomy. We were so careful. There were times he wanted to do it with me without wearing protection, but I always insisted. Except there was this one time..."

"Go on."

"I've racked my brain and this is the only time that I can think that we slipped up. Do you remember when you went to your lake house for a week?"

"You mean when my parents were here and they went with me."

"Well, you gave me the key to your house here. Jacque had gone back to France for two weeks. When he got back I asked him to meet me over here on his lunch hour. My God, Alicia when we saw each other we were just like animals. I had so missed him. We were all over each other. We didn't even get undressed. As soon as he walked in the door we started kissing. The next thing I knew, we were on the floor and he was in me. We thought that he stopped in time, but I guess not. I think that's when it happened."

"Don't you think you should tell him?"

Virginia reached for the wine bottle and filled her own glass one more time. "I think he's made it pretty clear that he doesn't want anything else to do with me. He's probably already found some other married woman up in Raleigh to service him. God, I've been a complete idiot."

"What does Henry want you to do?"

"I think his only concern is that I not do anything that will humiliate him or the girls. Beyond that I don't think he gives a damn. Alicia, you should see the way he looks at me. He gives me these cold stares. It's as though he is looking right through me. I mean, it's like I don't even exist. He's just so hurt and so angry."

"Does he threaten you? Has he hit you?"

"Henry's not like that. He's made it clear what he expects of me. He's also made it clear what the repercussion will be if I don't meet his demands. He's moved into the guest room. Our meal times are forced. Our conversations are brief and unemotional. I'm really afraid the girls are going to figure out that something is wrong."

"But he wants to stay married to you."

"I'm not sure he knows what he wants. Sometimes I can hear him crying. Alicia, I've really hurt him. I think I've destroyed the only man that really did love me."

"I should have been a better friend to you."

"You have been a good friend."

"No, I really haven't. A friend tells you what you want to hear. A good friend tells you what you need to hear. Virginia, when you first asked me to loan you my lake house so you could sleep with Jacque, I should have challenged you."

"What do you mean?"

Alicia lit another cigarette and exhaled the smoke through her nose. She studied Virginia's face. "From where I was sitting, it looked to me like you had it made. You had the big house, the fancy car, two beautiful children, and a husband that seemed to take pretty good care of you. Maybe he wasn't the most romantic man in town, but it looked to me like he was a pretty good catch. There must be a thousand women right here in Falls City that would have traded places with you in a heartbeat. Hell, Virginia, I would've traded places with you. I thought you knew what you were doing. I should have forced you to consider all that you were risking."

Tears streamed down Virginia's cheeks. "Then why didn't you? Why didn't you make me think this through? Why didn't you help me see that Jacque was just a player? He's a loser. Even if he'd wanted to marry me, I would never have been happy on a museum director's salary. I was crazy, Alicia. I was absolutely certifiable. I needed you to tell me the truth. You could have stopped me from making this horrible mistake."

Alicia's face grew stern. She tamped out her cigarette in the ashtray on the table in front of her. "Now, you just hold on for one damn minute, Missy! Don't you try to blame your mistake on me. You were worse than a dog in heat. You would have done whatever you had to do to get in bed with that Frenchman. I was just trying to help you get what I thought you wanted. And don't you forget it, Girlie, Henry didn't look all that good to you when you were taking your clothes off for Jacque."

Virginia wiped her eyes with a tissue. She got up and walked over to the kitchen sink, opened the sink cabinet, and tossed the tissue in the waste basket. "You're right. It wasn't your fault, but damn it…oh, what's the use? It's just that I do so wish you'd helped me think it all through."

"Okay, that's fair enough. I'll admit to letting you down in that area. I guess I was afraid that if I did you'd reject me. Virginia, you're a beautiful society lady. I was flattered you wanted to be my friend."

"And you're about the only friend I've got left that I can trust."

A smile crossed Alicia's face. "I've got to ask you. Was the sex really that good?"

Virginia nodded. "God, I don't know what it was. The chemistry between us was just unbelievable. I don't know if it was the sneaking around or just what, but when we got together…I mean…well…it was all about the sex. Sometimes we'd do it three or four times in one afternoon. He was like an addiction. I just kept wanting more and more."

"Wow! But now you don't think it was worth it?"

Virginia shook her head. More tears welled up in her eyes, rolled down her cheeks and dripped onto her blouse. "Just look at me. Look at the mess I've made of my marriage. My entire life is in ruins. What do you think?" Virginia laid her head down on the table as great sobs rocked her entire body. When she regained her composure she looked at Alicia. "I had to go over to Savannah and get some prescriptions from a psychiatrist there. I'm taking some kind of anti-anxiety tablet to try to calm me down during the day and a sleeping pill to help me sleep at night."

"Did you tell the shrink that you're pregnant?"

"I really didn't know I was at the time."

"Do you want to smoke a joint? It might do more to mellow you out than all the pills you can take. "

"You can if you want, but I'd better not."

"Virginia, I hate to point out the obvious to you, but we've already emptied two bottles of wine along with all the pills that you're popping. I think it's a bit late to think about your baby."

"No, it's not that. It's just that I need a clear head. I need you to help me make a plan. I really want you to be a good friend this time. Don't you dare just be a friend. I need you to be a really good friend. Tell me what I need to hear and not what you think I want to hear."

"Oh, like a couple of bottles of wine will give us both real clear heads?"

"No, but they have helped numb the pain."

Alicia stood walked to her wine rack. What the hell, if two bottles have numbed your pain then three ought to put us both in a coma. How about a bottle of red?"

"I really need your help. I need to get this taken care of, but I can't do it here in Falls City."

"Then let's go up to Atlanta."

"Will you help me make the arrangements?"

"Virginia...since I've come this far with you I guess I can go all the way."

"Will you go with me?"

Alicia nodded. "And now..." Alicia smiled, "How about that joint?"

This time it was Virginia that nodded.

CHAPTER 16

Steele stood at the nursery door. Randi was sitting on the floor playing a card game with Travis. They were playing Go Fish. Amanda was close by in a baby seat. She was awake and looking at the mobile that Randi had attached to the seat and was hanging directly above Amanda's head. Travis surprised Steele by leaning over and kissing Amanda on her forehead several times. That brought a big smile to Randi's face. Steele folded his arms and leaned against the door frame. He felt like the luckiest man in the world. His beautiful wife was radiant. His two children were healthy and happy. He whispered a prayer of thanksgiving to God.

"Steele, I didn't hear you come in."

"Daddy! Daddy!" Travis ran to Steele with outstretched arms. Steele picked him up and gave him a big squeeze. "Hey, Buddy, how's it going?"

"We're playing Go Fish. Guess what, Daddy? I'm winning."

"That's great, Travis. You must be a really good player. Mommy's pretty hard to beat."

Travis nodded his big smile and then started wiggling out of his arms in order to get down. "Books, Daddy...you promised me we'd read some books."

"Okay, go get a book."

Travis ran down the hallway toward his room. Steele knelt down on the floor between Randi and Amanda. He kissed Randi on the lips and then Amanda on the cheek. "And how are the two most beautiful girls in the entire world?"

Before Randi could answer, Travis came running back into the room with his arms full of books. He ran directly to Steele and sat down in his lap. "Let's read, Daddy."

"Whoa, there fellow... Just how many books do you have there? Let's count them." Steele counted out fourteen books. "Tell you what, how about you choose your favorite three books?"

"No, Daddy. I want to read all of them."

Steele chuckled. "Okay, we'll read them all, but you have to choose which ones to start with. So let's spread them out on the floor and you put them in the order that you want to read them. While you're doing that I want to talk to Mommy for a minute."

"Mommy's been crying."

"Oh?" Steele looked over at Randi. "While you're arranging your books, Mommy and I are going to step across the hall to our bedroom so that I can get out of my work clothes. I'll be back in just a minute so that we can read your books."

"Okay, Daddy."

Steele stood and gave Randi his hand to help her up off the floor. He picked up Amanda in her carrier and they went into the master bedroom. He unbuttoned his collar and started removing his clergy shirt. "Have you been having a rough day?"

Tears welled up in Randi's eyes. She opened the drawer of the lamp table next to her side of the bed. She handed Steele the real estate flyers that she had been given earlier in the day.

"What are these?"

"Mrs. Smythe and Mrs. Dexter came by earlier. They gave them to me. They said that these are the houses that the Altar Guild has chosen for us. They said that we could buy any one of the three."

Steele sat down on the side of the bed and studied the flyers. Randi sat next to him. "Honey, these aren't even near the type of house that we've been talking about. They're not even in the area of town that we want to live in."

"I know, Steele. Do we have to choose from one of these? I mean… can they do that? We didn't agree to let the Altar Guild choose our house. If we'd moved to San Antonio they were going to let us pick out our own house."

Steele shook his head. He reached over and took Randi's hand. "Listen to me. There's just been some sort of miscommunication. Let's give the Altar Guild the benefit of the doubt. They were just trying to help us. I'll straighten it all out with the Vestry. We're going to choose the house that we buy with our money."

"But Steele, I don't think they see it that way."

"What way?"

"I don't think that they see it as our money. I think they see the salary they pay you as their money. Since it's their money they think they have a right to tell us how to spend it. Remember, we went through this with my car. We bought my car with money from my trust fund. Even at that, they still thought they had a right to tell us what kind of car to buy."

Steele put his arm around her and brought her close to him. "Randi, I know that you're right, but part of my job here is to help them begin to see us as people and not the hired help. I have to help them understand that while I'm a priest I'm also a professional. They are compensating me for services rendered. I am not a feudal servant indebted to them for my livelihood. I think they also need to understand that our home is not an extension of the parish parlor. I need to do it not just for us, but for all the priests that will follow us here."

"I'm not sure you're going to be able to do all that."

Steele nodded, "You may be right, my little pessimist, but I'm going to give it a try. One thing I can promise you is this. We will be buying the house that we choose. No one at the church is going to pick it out for us."

Just then Travis came running into the room. His arms were once again filled with books. "Let's read, Daddy."

"Do you know which ones you want to start with?"

"Yes, Daddy." Travis handed Steele a book. "This one first."

"How about we sit up here on the bed? Do you think Amanda would like to read with us? You could sit on one side of me and we could put her on the other."

"Amanda can't read."

"That's right, she can't. But don't you think maybe she would like to hear your favorite stories?"

Travis nodded and began climbing up onto Steele and Randi's bed. "Okay, let's read."

Steele gathered his children on either side of him and began reading. By the time he had gotten halfway through the third book both of them were sleeping soundly.

CHAPTER 17

Steele, this is Rufus Petersen."

Steele's first thought was that someone was playing a joke on him. The voice on the other end of the telephone was warm and gentle. The Bishop usually barked his orders at Steele. He never called him by his first name and he always referred to himself as 'The Bishop'. He had never identified himself to Steele by his Christian name.

"I'm here in Falls City. Do you have any plans for lunch?"

Steele continued to be cautious. He still wasn't sure whether or not it was the Bishop. He was becoming increasingly suspicious that someone was playing a joke on him. Bishop Petersen never asked if he had plans. He always ordered him to cancel any plans he did have in order to accommodate the Bishop. The voice on the other end of the telephone continued. "If you don't have any plans, I'd like to buy your lunch. Now if you do, I understand. I can call your secretary and try to find another time that would work for you."

Steele decided to play along. "Gosh, Bishop Petersen, it's so nice to hear your voice. I do hope that you're feeling better. We've been praying for you." Steele felt a cringe of guilt. Then he smiled. He was now certain that someone was playing a joke on him. He speculated that Horace Drummond had put someone up to making the phone call. He decided to let the game continue. "I don't have any plans at all. I'm quite free for lunch."

"That's just great. Would you mind meeting me at The Victorian? Would twelve noon work for you?"

Steele could not wait to see how far the prankster was going to take this before he revealed his true identity. He decided to call his bluff. "Twelve noon at The Victorian. I'll be there. I look forward to having lunch with you...Bishop."

"I'll see you then." The telephone line was silenced.

Steele hung up the phone and smiled. He then pushed the numbers on the intercom for Horace's office. "Okay, you've had your fun. Your stooge called me and I played along, but I won't be meeting you for lunch."

"Brother, what are you talking about?"

Steele chuckled. "You know exactly what I'm talking about. You had someone call me pretending to be the Bishop. He asked me to meet him at The Victorian for lunch."

"Steele, I didn't ask anyone to call you."

"You serious?"

"As serious as a heart attack."

"Do you think I really did get a telephone call from Petersen?"

"There's only one way to find out."

Steele was still suspicious. "Okay, but let me tell you one thing, Horace Drummond, if I get over there and find out that you've played a practical joke on me, I will get even."

Horace let out his great baritone laugh. "You know, I think you might need a vacation. You're getting paranoid. When you get back, be sure and let me know who you had lunch with." Steele could hear him laughing as he hung up the telephone.

The Victorian is a restaurant at the end of Main Street in downtown Falls City. It's only a few blocks from First Church. It's aptly named since it's an old Victorian house that had been restored and converted into a dining facility. It is located on a beautiful corner lot underneath some large live oak trees and surrounded by dogwoods and azaleas. It's known for fine cuisine and excellent service. The prices on the menu insure an exclusive clientele. It was a gorgeous day in Falls City so Steele decided to walk the three blocks to the restaurant. When he arrived the maitre'd asked if he had a reservation. "No, I'm meeting someone. May I look for him?"

"Do you know who you're meeting? Perhaps they made a reservation?"

"Well, actually, I'm supposed to meet my Bishop. Have you seen a man with a purple clergy shirt on?"

The maitre'd shook his head. "No one by that description has arrived."

"Then someone is playing a practical joke on me. I'll just take a look around and see if I can discover who it is."

"Certainly, as you like."

Steele walked into the first dining room and looked around. He recognized a couple of the diners, but no one looked like they were waiting on him. He moved from room to room in the house with the same results. He was just about to leave when he saw a silver headed man at a corner table waving at him. At first he didn't recognize the man and then he realized that it really was the Bishop.

"Bishop, gosh, I didn't recognize you. You are mere shadow of your former self. How much weight have you lost?"

The Bishop stood and extended his hand to Steele. The two men shook hands. "Please be seated. I'm so glad that you could join me for lunch." The Bishop was wearing slacks, a sports shirt and a sports coat. Steele had never seen him in anything but a purple clergy shirt. He and Horace used to joke that Bishop Petersen probably slept in his purple shirt in a purple bed. Little did they know just how accurate their description had been. "A couple of heart attacks have a way of motivating you to lose some weight."

"You look great. You look ten years younger."

"Steele, you don't mind if I call you Steele?"

"No, I don't mind at all."

"And I want you to call me Rufus. We'll save the titles for formal occasions."

"Okay..." Steele was struggling to take in the Bishop's change of attitude.

"Before we go any further I want to clear up one thing. I owe you an apology. In fact, I owe you several apologies. You received my letter about your compensation right before I got sick."

"Yes."

"I should never have written that letter. I was just upset and if the truth be told I was envious."

"Bishop..."

"Please, we're having a conversation man to man. Please, call me Rufus."

"Okay, Rufus. I want you to know that I did not ask First Church for a single thing."

"I know that now. It's just that you already were making more than the Bishop of this Diocese and this new compensation package puts you so far ahead of me."

"There's another way to look at it Bish...Rufus. Maybe the Rector of First Church isn't being overpaid. Maybe you're being underpaid."

Rufus shook his head. "I've always known that the Rector of First Church's compensation would be driven by that of the Headmaster of the school. They tend to demand better salaries than most parish priests. I understood that the parish would want to keep their Rector's package a little higher than that of the man working for him. On the other hand, I have to be careful not to get the Bishop's salary too far beyond that of the mission clergy and the Rectors of the smaller parishes in the Diocese. But that's not the reason for this lunch. I invited you to lunch so that we could turn over a new leaf. You and I have not been able to get along since you came to this Diocese. I confess that most of that has been my fault. I want to start over. I want to be your friend as well as your Bishop."

"I appreciate that. I appreciate that a lot. I continue to be very close to my last Bishop. I'd hoped we could have that kind of relationship."

"I hope that we can as well."

The waiter came and the two men ordered their lunch. The Bishop ordered a small salad with the dressing on the side. He wanted his fish broiled, no butter on it, and steamed vegetables. He wanted his tea to be unsweetened. "I admire your discipline. I hope you won't be offended if I order a Reuben sandwich."

Rufus Petersen let out such a roar of laughter that the other patrons in the restaurant all turned to look at him.

Steele was embarrassed. "What's so funny?"

"Steele, a Reuben sandwich is the last thing I ate immediately before I had my heart attack."

"I'm so sorry. I had no idea. Perhaps I should order something else."

"Nonsense, enjoy your sandwich. Just realize that the day is coming when grilled fish and steamed vegetables will be your daily fare as well."

Through the lunch Steele listened carefully as Rufus cleansed his conscience. He confessed that he should have been more supportive of Steele during his investigation of the embezzlement. He had just been listening to the wrong people at First Church, but that was going to change. He told Steele about his near death experience. He rehearsed for him his conversation with his mother. He told him how he was trying to make amends with all the priests that he felt like he'd let down. Then he surprised Steele with a question. "Is there some project we could work on together? I would like the Diocese to partner with First Church on some good work for the poor and needy."

"I do have something that I'm working on right now, but I'm not sure that it's something the Diocese will want to support."

"Now that sounds ominous."

"It's really not. It's a need not just in Falls City but for the entire region. I want to do something to help some teenagers that no one else is doing anything to assist."

"Tell me more."

Steele studied the Bishop's face. "Do you have any plans after lunch?"

"No, I was just going to drive back up to Savannah."

"Tell you what. Let's go back over to my office. I have a meeting scheduled with Horace Drummond and a couple of other people. I'd like for you to meet them. Let's start there."

The Bishop paid the check. Steele couldn't help but notice that he left a very generous tip. He then followed him to the parking lot where the valet delivered the Bishop's Cadillac. "I'm trying to make a lot of changes in my life, but I just can't bring myself to give up my Cadillac."

"Bishop, you spend a lot of time in your car traveling around this Diocese visiting your congregations. That's a lot of driving and a lot of miles each week. I really don't think anyone envies you your Cadillac."

The Bishop smiled and handed Steele the keys. "You drive."

CHAPTER 18

The Women's Center for Health and Family Planning was located on a side street in an industrial park in Atlanta. It was out of the way, so Alicia and Virginia felt that it would be safe and they could protect their anonymity. Just to make sure they each wore a disguise complete with wigs, ball caps, and sunglasses. Alicia borrowed a neighbor's car for the trip. When they arrived, neither of them were prepared for the demonstrators standing on the opposite side of the street. They were carrying signs. The signs were imprinted with messages condemning abortion. Some had Bible quotes on them. Others had large portraits of aborted fetuses. When Alicia pulled the car up to the gate of the clinic's parking lot, a security guard came out and opened it for them. The demonstrators began shouting at them. "Don't do it! Please don't murder your baby!!! Your baby wants to live!!! You'll burn in hell if you do this!!!" Others dropped to their knees and began praying. Tears streamed down Virginia's cheeks. She buried her face in her hands.

Virginia paid cash for the abortion. The receptionist that took her money did not greet her or ask her any questions. She simply handed her some documents to sign and escorted her to a room at the end of the hallway and closed the door behind her. The procedure was so impersonal. The doctor performing the abortion never even made eye contact with her. The nurses went about their duties in a robotic fashion. The clinic speakers blared music at a volume just loud enough to drown out the sounds of the demonstrators outside.

Virginia decided to lie down in the back seat of the car for the ride back to Falls City. She was weak. She just wanted to sleep. As Alicia pulled the car out of the parking lot and back onto the street, the demonstrators began yelling at them. Virginia could hear them. "Murderer!! The fires of hell are waiting on you!! Baby Killer!!! Baby Killer!!!" They began to chant in unison.

When they were out of the industrial park, Alicia looked back over her shoulder at Virginia. "You okay?"

Virginia nodded again.

"I need a drink. You want one?"

Virginia nodded.

"Here." Alicia handed her a silver flask filled with vodka.

"That was just awful! The demonstrators made me feel bad enough, but those robots in that clinic couldn't have been more impersonal."

"They were a bunch of ice people. You got that one right. How long until you're back to your old self?"

"Well, from what I could pry out of them I should be feeling close to normal by the time we get back to Falls City." Virginia took another swallow from the flask and then handed it to Alicia. She did the same. Alicia pulled the car onto the freeway and headed south. "Do you think I'm going to go to hell for what I've done?"

"Oh Virginia, don't pay any attention to those religious nuts."

Virginia sat up in the back seat. "Alicia, I need you to be a really good friend right now. Don't tell me what you think I want to hear. Tell me the truth. Am I going to go to hell?"

Alicia set the cruise control on the car. "Good God, I don't know. I don't even know if there is a hell."

Virginia began sobbing.

"Oh crap, girl. I'm really getting tired of your tears. You're bringing me down. Now knock it off. Let's listen to the radio or something."

"I'm sorry, Alicia. It's just that I've made such a mess of my life."

"Okay, you want me to be a really good friend. You're right. You've made some really stupid choices. You've messed up a marriage that most every woman in the entire State of Georgia would trade her soul for. You screwed on your husband with an absolute loser who just happened to have a pretty face. You've risked your reputation and the respect of your children. And you've absolutely destroyed the only man who probably will ever completely love you. Now do you feel better?"

"No, but thank you very much."

"Virginia, you've had to do what you had to do. You really had no other choice. Henry may not ever forgive you, but he sure as hell wouldn't forgive you if you had given birth to another man's baby."

"Adulterer! Murderer! Liar! Slut!" Virginia screamed out the words as she began pounding her legs with her fists. She was out of control. Over and over she pounded her knees. She shouted. "Slut! Slut! Slut!" She was sobbing and yelling at the same time. She was moving all over the back seat as though she were having convulsions.

Alicia pulled the car to the side of the road and ran around to the back door. She opened the door and grabbed Virginia's arms. "Stop it! Stop it! Get control of yourself." She slapped Virginia across the cheek. "This is not helping." She screamed at Virginia over the noise of a passing semi. Virginia collapsed into her arms as the hysteria poured out of her. Alicia embraced her and held on to her until she finally relaxed. "I was afraid of something like this." She reached into her coat pocket and brought out a prescription bottle. She opened it and handed a pill to Virginia. Here, wash it down with this. She gave her the silver flask. Virginia took the pill, put it in her mouth, and then drank from the flask.

"What did you give me?"

"It's something that's going to help you sleep the rest of the way home. It's also going to give me some peace and quiet."

Virginia lay down in the back seat. "You're a really good friend, Alicia."

Alicia patted her. "I know, but I can make you one promise that you can take to the bank. And this is your really good friend talking. If you ever make any more stupid decisions, you'll be minus one friend of any kind. I'm not going through anything like this with you ever again." Her words went unheard. Virginia was already sleeping soundly.

CHAPTER 19

"What do you have to report?" Henry Mudd reached for the manila folder that his private detective was handing him. The detective took a seat opposite Henry's desk. "I just got a call from one of my agents up in Atlanta. He followed them to an abortion clinic. He's convinced that she had it done."

Henry nodded and opened the folder. "Has she been in contact with that Frenchman?"

"She called him while you were in Las Vegas."

Henry smiled a knowing smile. "I figured she'd use that opportunity to try to get in touch with him."

She bought a prepaid telephone card at a drug store. Then she went to a pay phone and called him. That's the only call she made to him."

"Could you hear anything?"

"That's the wonderful thing about our equipment. It's so sensitive we could hear everything. We even could hear his side of the conversation. There's a transcript in the file. I also have the tape if you want it."

"Give me the bottom line on their conversation. Did she tell him about the baby?"

"No, she didn't tell him she was pregnant. The conversation was pretty cold. Clearly he has no further interest in her. If fact, he told her to get on with her life. Since she initiated the call, I can't tell you what she'd hoped to hear from him."

"Anything else?"

"We have a recording of her visit over at Alicia Thompson's house. They spent the afternoon drinking wine and smoking pot."

"What did you hear?"

"Not much that you don't already know. She realizes she's messed up her life and that she's hurt you badly."

"And what did Alicia have to say?"

"Kind of interesting. As you can hear for yourself, she came down on her pretty hard at one point in the conversation."

"That's something she should have done before she started covering for her to jump in the sack with that frog. What about Alicia? I want her to pay for what she's done. Do you have any ideas?"

"I'm working on it. She seems to be living off some sort of inheritance her daddy left her. It's not much, but then she lives pretty simply. She has a no-good boyfriend that's somewhat of a pothead himself. They don't live together. They just get together every now and then for sex and then go their separate ways."

"What about her dealer? Where does she get her pot?"

"She has several sources. A couple of them are pretty upstanding folks in the community. One is a member of your church."

"Let's set up a sting. Let's have the police catch her with a stash, but make sure it's more that a few ounces. Do you think we could plant some other substances in her house? I want to hurt her and I want to hurt her bad. I don't want her getting off with a fine. I think the next house she has to loan out for adulterers should be a women's correctional facility."

"You're the boss. I can get anything done for a price."

"Money is no object. Just set it up. Now what about the frog?"

The detective began chuckling. "Man, he's a real piece of work. He couldn't get out of Falls City fast enough after a couple of my boys had a little talk with him."

"I saw those guys. Where did you find that muscle? I'd run the other direction if those two goons even looked at me. They're gigantic."

"Like I said, it's just a matter of price."

"Where is he now?"

"He's up in Raleigh. He got a job as an actor in a dinner theatre. It must not pay very well because he's staying in a flop house in a seedy section of town."

"That sounds a bit too good for him. Let's hit him again. I want that fool to think twice before he beds another man's wife."

"You're too late!"

"What do you mean too late?"

"He's found another one. That's what I mean. He's bedding the wife of a C.E.O. of a big insurance company up there."

"Are you kidding me?"

The detective smiled broadly and reached into his briefcase. "I've been saving the best for last." He placed a large manila envelope on Henry's desk. "Have a look at these."

Henry opened the envelope and let out a low whistle. "You guys are really good. These pictures are so clear. How'd you get these shots?"

"We used the same camera set-up we did with your wife. It's just amazing how careless two people in heat can be. They think they're being so clever, but...well...I guess these are just proof we're a lot smarter."

"Does the woman's husband know?"

"Not from what we can tell. I think it's the same scenario as yours. The poor sap is lumbering through life thinking he has it made while his darling little wife is out there spreading her legs for another man."

"Let's hit that Frenchman in a way that he won't ever forget. I want him brought down so hard this time that he'll be on the next plane back to France."

"What do you propose?"

"I have three things in mind."

"Before you list your proposals, I need to caution you about a part of the conversation between Alicia and your wife."

"Go on."

"Well, you'll hear for yourself. Your wife described for Alicia the sex between her and the Frenchman. I don't think you're going to like what you hear. I know if I was in your shoes I wouldn't."

Henry sat back in his chair. He gritted his teeth. He could feel his fist tighten. The anger raged inside him. "Here's what I want you to do. First, send these pictures to this woman's husband. Make sure that you enclose a note identifying the frog, his employment address and the address of his flop house. Have your man hand them directly to the husband. Don't run any chance that some well meaning secretary or his wife intercepts them."

"No problem, what is the second thing you want done?"

"I want you to find out just who the money is behind that dinner theatre. Pay them a little visit. Tell them that you're an attorney. Show them the pictures and tell them that unless they fire that frog on the spot the husband is going to file a lawsuit against them."

"That worked with the museum board here. It should work up there. Now, I can hardly wait to hear the third thing you want done."

Henry leaned forward across his desk. He indicated for the detective to do the same. He lowered his voice to just above a whisper. "I want you to send your muscle up there to see that Frenchman again. This time I don't want them to just talk to him. This time I want those goons to work him over. Make sure they pay special attention to the area between his legs. If they do their job right, that little creep will never again be able to bed another man's wife. And I want to make sure he never sires any more bastard babies again. When they're finished with him have them stuff one of these pictures of him and this woman and one of him and Virginia in his pocket."

Henry sat back in his chair and looked at the detective. The detective did the same. He shook his head.

"Have I gone too far? Is that more than your boys are willing to do?"

"No, they'll do it, but it's really going to cost you."

"Do you want that in cash?"

The detective stood and extended his hand to Henry. "Cash will do nicely." He turned to leave.

"One more thing, keep your boys on Virginia. I want to know her every move."

"Consider it done."

The detective left and Henry looked at the pictures of the Frenchman and the other man's wife. The anger welled up in him again. He leaned down to put them in his bottom desk drawer when he noticed a very pretty pair of feminine legs standing at the end of his desk. He followed them all the way up a beautifully proportioned body until his eyes met those of a gorgeous young woman. "Who are you?"

"I'm sorry, Mister Mudd. I hope I didn't startle you. I'm your new receptionist. The office manager hired me yesterday. He thought I should come down and introduce myself to you at the first opportunity. She extended her hand, "Hi, I'm Dee."

Henry took her hand and shook it. He stood so that he could get a better look at her. "Dee, is that really you're name?"

"Yes sir, it's short for Delilah, just like the woman in the Bible."

"The one that cut Sampson's hair?"

"Yes sir, but I don't cut hair. I just answer the telephone. I hope that you'll let me know if I can do anything for you."

Henry studied her face. She had gorgeous sparkling eyes and a brilliant smile with perfect teeth. "You can count on that, Dee. I'll let you know if there's anything that you can do for me."

"Well, thank you for letting me work here."

"I'm glad you're here. Welcome."

Dee turned and walked out of his office. Henry stood watching her. Then to his surprise he realized that he was beginning to have some very pleasant stirrings. These sensations came on very rare occasions since he'd discovered his wife's adultery. A broad smile crossed Henry Mudd's face.

CHAPTER 20

When Steele got back to his office, he found that Horace Drummond and two young men were waiting on him. "Bishop, you remember Doctor Drummond."

"Yes, of course I do." The Bishop extended his hand to Horace.

"Bishop I almost didn't recognize you. My goodness, you're the picture of health."

"Thank you. A couple of heart attacks will give you a lot of motivation for diet and exercise."

"Well, I hope Almeda doesn't get a look at you. The woman is riding me all the time about losing some weight and getting a trainer."

"Well, maybe you should listen to her." The Bishop patted Horace on his protruding stomach. "Doctor Drummond, I just wanted to tell you what a wonderful job I think you're doing. Steele has been telling me all about the good outreach ministries you are overseeing for First Church."

Horace shot a questioning look at Steele. Steele gave him a knowing smile. "Thank you, Bishop. I think that we're really helping a lot of people in dire circumstances."

"I know that you are. I have no doubt about it."

"And who are these two young gentlemen?" The Bishop gushed.

"These are the young men I wanted you to meet. Bishop Petersen, I would like to have you meet Bud and Justin."

The Bishop extended his hand to each of the young men. "It's so nice to meet you. I always enjoy meeting the youth leaders in my Diocese."

This time it was the two boys that gave Steele a questioning look. "These young men are not leaders in our youth work, Bishop. They are some of the young men I want us to help."

"Oh?"

"Let's all sit over here." Steele motioned toward the seating area in his office. "Horace, is Skipper going to join us?"

"He's running a bit late, but he'll be here." Horace looked at the Bishop. "Bishop Petersen, Skipper Hodges is the director of the homeless shelter here in Falls City."

"You're not trying to tell me that these fine young men are homeless, are you, Steele?"

Steele smiled, "Well, they were. Bud was homeless, but he's now living with Horace and Almeda. Justin is still living in the shelter."

"I see," Bishop Petersen looked at each of the boys. They were clean-cut from what he could see. Bud was particularly well groomed. Justin was wearing a very tight white tee shirt with some even tighter jeans. The Bishop thought that they may have actually belonged to the boy's sister. Justin also had an earring in his ear, a bracelet on his arm, and several rings on his fingers. "Did you boys run away from home?"

As both boys blushed a bright red, Steele came to their rescue. "No, Bishop, they didn't run away from home. I'll let them tell you their stories for themselves."

Just then there was a knock on Steele's office door. Skipper Hodges opened the door. "Your secretary said it was okay for me to come on in."

"You bet, Skipper. I'm just so glad that you could join us. We're just getting started. "Bishop, this is Skipper Hodges. We mentioned him to you earlier. Skipper, this is Bishop Petersen."

The Bishop stood and shook his hand. "Please do join us. These young men were just about to tell me about themselves."

Bud told the Bishop his story first. He told him about his mother walking in on him with a gay friend. He told him about how his dad beat him and how his mother packed his clothes and then threw him out of the house. He told him about living on the streets and under the Falls River Bridge. He confessed that he had earned money by servicing some of the married men in the park bathroom. He had been living on the streets until Steele could get him a cot in Skipper's shelter. He didn't have to stay there long because Almeda and Horace had taken him under their wings. He was now in school and his grades were better than they had ever been in his life. He said Horace and Almeda were the best parents he's ever had.

"That's quite a story. Is there anything else you want to tell me?"

"Yes, sir. I'd like to tell you about what they did to my friend Kevin." He then told him about his friend Kevin and how he stabbed his father in self-defense. But even though it was self-defense he is now in a juvenile correctional facility.

"And all this happened to you and your friend because the two of you have chosen to be homosexuals?"

"I'd like to answer that." Skipper was obviously upset. "Bishop, I don't believe these young men have chosen their sexuality. Frankly, I don't think anyone gets to choose. People don't get to choose whether or not they're born to be left-handed or right-handed. And I don't think they get to choose their sexuality either. Every respectable medical, psychological and psychiatric organization believes that sexuality is predetermined."

The Bishop nodded, "Well, I'm not up on all these things. Let me ask my question again. You boys are homeless because you're homosexuals, right?"

Steele smiled, "I think these young men prefer to be described as gay. Of course, they would prefer just to be recognized for who they are and not be categorized at all."

"Yes, of course. I apologize." The Bishop chuckled. "I fear I'm out of step. I need to learn all the language of political correctness when it comes to these things."

"No problem." Bud smiled. "I'm still getting use to the label myself."

The Bishop looked over at Justin. "Justin, isn't it?"

"Yes, sir."

"Would you like to tell me your story?"

"Yes, sir." Justin took a deep breath. "My story is a little different than Bud's story. I'm a little older than Bud. I'm nineteen. I'm from North Carolina. It's a tiny little town, so I doubt if you've ever heard of it."

"What's it near?"

"Maggie Valley."

"I know the area. Lot's of mountains around there."

"Yes, sir. It's really beautiful. We lived in a very rural area."

"Go ahead."

"Well, I've known all my life that I was different. I mean, just look at me. I can't help the way I walk or move or talk. I know that I'm not like most guys."

"But Bud, you don't..." The Bishop looked confused. "I mean, you look like you could be an Olympic swimmer."

Justin leaned forward in his chair. "Bishop, that's probably one of the biggest misconceptions. Everyone thinks that we all act like sissies. I know lots of gay guys that are really masculine. You'd never suspect them."

The Bishop shrugged. "I think I have a lot to learn."

"I think that Justin here will help you understand that his physical mannerisms have brought a lot of grief into his life." Skipper interjected. "Go on with your story, Justin."

"As I was saying, Bishop, I've known all my life that I was different. I wasn't any good at anything the other boys in my school could do. I run like a girl. I couldn't play ball, hell…" He stopped and blushed. "I'm sorry."

"It's okay, Justin." Steele reassured him. "The Bishop has heard that word before. I've even heard him use it in a couple of sermons. On occasion, he even suggested unless I did something to change my ways, it just might be my future residence." Steele winked at the Bishop.

The Bishop smiled at Steele and nodded. "Well, no longer, Father Austin…no longer." The Bishop looked back at Justin. "Just tell your story in your own words, young man."

"Anyway, all the other kids made fun of me all the time. Everyone wanted to beat me up. The boys would hide and throw rocks at me. They called me *Sissy.*" Rufus Petersen remembered that his schoolyard life was not much different. He was a fat little boy. The other boys made fun of him because of his weight. He, too, was subjected to name calling and beatings. Only his torture did not end with elementary school, it followed him all the way to boarding school. He found himself identifying with Justin. His heart was going out to him.

"My dad actually seemed to take delight in the beatings that I got." Justin continued. "He used to tell me that they would toughen me up. He was always trying to make a man out of me."

The Bishop was now nodding his head. He was really listening to the young man. Horace shot Steele a knowing look and nodded toward the Bishop. Steele acknowledged that he had received his message with a slight smile and nod of his own. "When did your parents realize that you were gay?" The Bishop asked.

"They've never acknowledged that I am gay." Justin shook his head. "They prefer to call me a queer and a sinner."

"So that's how you ended up on the streets?" The Bishop asked.

"There's more to it than that." Justin was now sitting forward on the sofa. He was looking down at the floor. His hands were folded in front of him. "I went to a pretty small country school. All the grades shared one building. We had a wrestling team. There was this senior on the wrestling team that really liked me. He would pick me up in his car and we'd go to the movies, bowling, and things like that. He was really muscular and real good looking. My dad was happy that I had him for a friend. He kept saying that he hoped that Rocky would be a good influence on me. Rocky was so masculine that no one suspected that he was gay. One summer afternoon we went skinny dipping in the creek. We didn't think anyone was around. After we swam for a while we lay down on this big rock and started making love. A game warden checking fish licenses walked up on us. He arrested us and took us over to the sheriff's office. It was a big scandal in our little town."

Justin stopped and wiped his eyes. "My family is real religious. They took me to the preacher. They had a special service to pray that Jesus would heal me. The preacher tried to exorcise me of my Sodomite Demon. They then sent me to a camp that the preacher knew about. It was supposed to make sure that the Demon would never enter my body again. The camp was run by some more preachers. At the camp they made us memorize a Bible passages forbidding men to lay with men. We had to recite them over and over again. They watched us all the time. We were never left alone, not even when we went to the bathroom. They even took turns watching us when we were sleeping. If they caught us with...well...uhr..." Justin blushed and looked over at Skipper with a pleading look.

Skipper came to his rescue. "You mean, if the preachers discovered that you were aroused."

He nodded. "Even if we were asleep, they would wake us up and beat us with belts. They would strip us down and beat our naked backs, bottoms, legs, and sometimes our stomachs and chests with belts. Then they would make us sit in bathtubs filled with ice. It was awful."

"Is that a true story?" The Bishop had a look of disbelief on his face. "I just can't believe that men of God would do that to you."

"Bishop, why would I lie to you? I don't really know you. I'm only telling you my story because Skipper asked me to." Then Justin stood up. "You know what? I don't care whether you believe me or not. I don't need this. I'm leaving."

Steele stood and took Justin's arm. "Please stay. I believe you. I just don't think Bishop Petersen has ever heard a story like yours before."

Bishop Petersen stood as well. "Yes, Justin. I didn't mean to offend you. It's just that your story is…well, son, you've really been through a living hell. Please sit back down. I want to hear more."

Justin nodded and sat back on the couch. "Well, there really isn't much more to tell. I managed to run away from the camp. I hitched it up to Atlanta. There I lived on the streets. I tried to get some odd jobs, but no one would hire me without an address and a telephone number. Like Bud here, I earned some money servicing some of the suits who came down to the bus station looking for sex. When it started turning cold in Atlanta, I made my way to Florida. Now I'm on my way back up there. Quite honestly, I can earn more money in Atlanta. Anyway, that's been my life for the past three years."

"Three years!" Bishop Petersen almost shouted. "You've been living like this for three years?"

"Yes, sir."

The Bishop sat in silence. Then he looked at Skipper. "Surely these young men are an exception. You don't see that many of them in a small town like Falls City?"

"Bishop, we have one room at the shelter reserved for teen males. It sleeps eight boys. Last night we turned away that same number."

"Are these the type of young men you want to help, Steele?"

"Yes, Bishop. Horace and his committee have been looking for a property we might convert into a safe house for gay teens that no longer have a home."

"Have you found anything, Horace?"

"We're still looking. There are zoning laws we have to consider, and then we also want it to be secure so as to insure the safety of the residents. The committee has come up with a handbook of policies for boys and girls that want to live in the house."

"Girls?" The Bishop shouted. Are you trying to tell me that there are parents that disown their daughters because they're gay? Is that the right word for them as well?"

Skipper answered the Bishop, "Yes, there are such parents. And yes, that word can be used for lesbians as well."

The Bishop sat in silence as though it was all just too much to absorb. "Go on. Tell me about these policies you're developing."

"You know…the usual stuff. They have to go to school, have part time jobs, be drug and alcohol-free, etcetera."

"What do you want to call it?"

Steele smiled. "I think we'll call it Rainbow House."

A puzzled looked crossed Rufus Petersen's face. He wrinkled his brow. "Why Rainbow House?"

"Well, the flag for the gay and lesbian movement is a rainbow flag." Steele replied.

"Are you trying to get these kids killed?"

This time it was Steele and Horace that shot each other puzzled looks. "Of course not, what makes you think we're trying to get them killed?"

"Steele, Horace, gentlemen—have you forgotten that you're opening this house in a small town in south Georgia? If you start flying a rainbow flag in front of that house, every religious nut in five counties is going to be over here picketing it and trying to shut it down. I don't need to tell you what the Klan will want to do to it."

Horace let out a low whistle. "Steele, he's right. The safety of these kids has to come first. We need to come up with another name. Do you have any ideas, Bishop?"

The Bishop shook his head. Everyone in the room began making suggestions, but nothing seemed to hit the mark. Then the Bishop stood. "I've got it. You were on the right track with your rainbow idea, but that's a bit too obvious. Let's be a little more subtle. It was Noah that first saw the rainbow in the sky. So what do you think about Noah's House?"

Bud replied first, "I like it."

Steele and the others smiled. "I think I like it too."

"I really don't care what we call it." Justin interjected. "I just want a home with my own room in it."

"That's the goal." Steele nodded. "Bishop, do you think this is something we can work on together?"

The Bishop began shaking everyone's hands. He began with the two teens. He followed his handshake by giving each of them a warm embrace. "I'll have to present it to the Diocesan Council first, but they'll approve it."

"You can't be sure of that, Bishop." Steele questioned. "I know some of the people on that council and they're pretty conservative."

Rufus Petersen stopped at the door and smiled back at Steele. "I may have had a spiritual awakening, Father Austin, but I'm still the Bishop that likes getting his way. Gentlemen, I will get my way in this matter as well. God bless you all."

CHAPTER 21

The atmosphere in the Vestry of First Church had been transformed since the first meeting Steele Austin had with them. At that time, there were virtually no friendly faces at the table. Stone Clemons and Chief Sparks were the only supportive voices he could count on. Howard Dexter, Henry Mudd, Ned Boone, and the remaining members of the Vestry were opposed to Steele and every aspect of his vision for the parish. Now things were different, but not perfect. Henry Mudd was now united with Stone and the Chief in their support for Steele's ministry. Howard Dexter could be won over, but his final vote was always dependent on the dollars being expended. He preferred to have First Church dollars deposited in his little bank and left there for all eternity. Stone Clemons had told Steele that Howard Dexter had a cash register where his heart was supposed to be. Steele had learned that his characterization was pretty accurate.

Elmer Idle was a new member of the Vestry. He was the husband of one of Steele's staff members, Judith. Steele had encouraged Elmer to run for the Vestry before he discovered just how disloyal Judith was to him. She tried to undermine him at every opportunity, both with her fellow staff members and the members of the parish. The remaining members of the Vestry tended to follow the lead of the others.

"Gentlemen, if you would please take the copy of the agendas that were mailed to you last week. You'll notice that we have two items in particular to consider." Steele looked around the table. All members were present, including his Chancellor, Stone Clemons. Just then the conference room door opened and Ned Boone entered. "Good evening, Mister Boone. Did you wish to speak with the Vestry this evening?"

Ned Boone frowned at Steele. "No, I do not. I was under the impression that these meetings are open to members of the congregation."

"Yes, sir, they are." "Steele forced a smile. "You are certainly welcome to observe. We have no secrets."

Ned Boone took a seat in one of the chairs next to the wall of the conference room. Steele handed him a copy of the agenda. "I don't need one. I already have a copy of the agenda."

Steele glanced over at Elmer Idle. Elmer avoided Steele's eyes and looked down at the table and blushed. Steele then knew where Ned Boone had gotten his copy of the agenda. "The first item on the agenda concerns a safe house for homeless teens that we want to start here in Falls City. If you'll look in your packets, Horace and I mailed you all the background materials on this particular project. As you can see for yourselves, the need is well established. This project would be sponsored by the Chadsworth Alexander Endowment, the Diocese, and this parish."

Howard Dexter raised his hand, "Misturh Austin, I'm curious as to why parish funds would be needed for this work? There should be sufficient income from the Chadsworth Alexander Endowment to support this endeavor. I would think that parish funds should be used for parish purposes."

Steele smiled, "Thank you for your question, Mister Dexter. The truth of the matter is that the remaining income from the Alexander Endowment has already been committed for the next three years. There's only enough to partially fund this project. The Bishop has committed to funding one third if the parish can fund the other."

Howard Dexter returned Steele's smile. "Misturh Austin, I'm sure this is a very worthwhile project and it pleases me to know that the Diocese would be willing to commit funds to it. A partnership with the Diocese would be a star in our crown. But Misturh Austin, I have some very serious reservations about committing parish funds to this endeavor for the next three years. Just how do you plan to fund it after the three years have passed?"

Steele had prepared himself for Howard Dexter's objections. He had anticipated his questions based on past experience with him. "Mister Dexter, the missions committee anticipates that the Soup Kitchen and the Medical Clinic will have sufficient fund raising income of their own in place over the next three years so that they will no longer need the income from the Alexander Endowment. That income can then be diverted to funding this project, thus relieving both this parish and the Diocese from having to support it further. We simply need the parish and the Diocese to pledge their money as seed money for three years."

Howard thumbed through the stack of papers on the table in front of him. "That sounds real nice, but Misturh Austin, my hunch is that over the next three years you'll be coming at us with even more projects for the poor that you'll want us to fund."

"Yes, sir, you're correct about that. As I stated to the congregation in my sermon a few weeks ago, it's my dream that this parish will become involved in several ministries to the poor and needy over the next few years."

"Well, Misturh Austin, we're not a wealthy parish. God has blessed us with some resources, but they are limited. We simply cannot do everything. We have to establish our priorities. It appears to me that our first priority is to take care of this parish. Personally, I would like to see any excess funds we have be directed toward our major repair fund or perhaps to our endowment for the cemetery."

Steele was trying his best not to let his frustration show. He had been through this line of argument with Howard Dexter before. He could almost anticipate his next question. He was hoping that Stone or Chief Sparks would say something. Then he looked over at the two of them. They were sitting opposite each other at the conference table. They both had Cheshire cat grins on their faces. It was then that Steele realized they were sitting back enjoying this exchange between Howard Dexter and him. He decided to bring their pleasure to an end. "Well, Misturh Dexter, I believe you have made some real good points. I guess that we should forget this project all together. I'll call the Bishop after the meeting and tell him that First Church won't be able to partner with the Diocese on this. Chief Sparks, will you make that motion and Stone, as Chancellor, will you second it?"

Steele smiled to himself as he saw the grins transform into a look of panic on his two friends faces. Chief Sparks spoke first. "Let's not be too hasty. I think the project is well worthwhile and could do a lot to help us remove the homeless teens from the streets in this city. Not only will it meet a need for the teens, but we in law enforcement believe it would help eliminate some of the crimes directly related to these homeless. Don't you think so, Stone?"

It suddenly came to Stone Clemons that the student had just become the teacher. He smiled a broad, approving smile at Steele. "Reverend Father, I agree with the Chief here. The project is worthwhile. While Misturh

Dexter's questions have a great deal of merit, I trust the various committees to do their work. If the Chief makes the motion that we make a three year commitment to this project, I'd be happy to second it."

"Before you do!" Ned Boone exploded. "May I speak?"

All the heads at the table jerked toward the outburst. Steele had experienced Ned Boone's temper before. He prepared himself for another. "Mister Boone, it appears the Vestry is all listening."

"Good, because there is something you gentlemen need to know. The thing that the Rector is not telling you is that this house is for a bunch of queers! He's planning on opening a house to teach these vulnerable teenagers how to be homosexuals. It's going to be nothing but a den of iniquity. He wants to turn our fair city into Sodom and Gomorrah. Instead of building them a house, he should be praying for their salvation."

"The Rector has not tried to hide any aspect of this project." It was Henry Mudd's voice. While Steele knew that he had Henry's total support he was really pleased to hear him speak up. "Ned, while I have a pretty good idea as to just where you got your copy of tonight's agenda…" Henry stopped and shot a look at Elmer Idle. Elmer did not meet his gaze, but continued to stare at the table. "Anyway, it would have been helpful if they had also given you a complete copy of the Vestry Packet for tonight. You would have been able to read all the background material for this ministry. You would have also seen for yourself that the Rector was upfront from the very first sentence as to just who will be living in this house. And I personally resent your characterization of this ministry and our Rector's intent for it."

Ned turned beet red. "Henry, are you trying to tell me that you, of all people, support this project for these sinners? It's just going to be one of those queer bath houses like they have up in Atlanta."

Henry pursed his lips and shook his head. "You know, Ned. I don't know if these young people are sexually confused, curious, mentally ill, or if they simply can't help themselves. I'm going to leave all that to smarter men than me. The one thing I do know is that these teenagers are homeless. They have no place to go. They're sleeping under bridges and on park benches. I agree with Father Austin. The least we can do is give them a safe place to sleep at night. As to whether or not they can be healed or cured or whatever, I'm leaving that to the shrinks and the preachers. I do agree with you that, like all of us, they need salvation, but I'm leaving that part to God." Henry smiled at Chief Sparks. "Chief, if you don't mind, I'd like to make the motion that the First Church Vestry make a commitment to support one-third of this ministry each year for the next three years."

Chief Sparks returned his smile. "I don't mind at all. And if my friend Stone agrees, I'll second it."

The motion passed with only Howard Dexter and Elmer Idle voting against it. Steele then called the Vestry's attention to the second item on the agenda. "As you can see, we need to finalize the housing allowance portion of my contract. According to our agreement, I would be granted the equivalent of the fair market value of the current Rectory. As you can see in your Vestry packet, I had three different realtors determine the fair market value of the Rectory. The three appraisals are in your packet. They are all within five thousand dollars of each other. I took the middle appraisal. I then asked three mortgage institutions to provide me with estimated mortgage payments for that amount, including taxes and insurance, just as the parish currently pays. I then took the average for utilities and maintenance over the past three years on the Rectory and added them to that total. I gave these numbers to the parish finance committee. They have approved that amount and are presenting it to you as their recommendation for my housing allowance."

Once again, it was Howard Dexter that raised his hand. "Misturh Austin, with all due respect, this number appears to be exorbitant. I would be absolutely embarrassed to have the members of the parish know that this Vestry had authorized this amount for a housing allowance for our Rector."

Steele felt his body tense. He wasn't prepared for Howard to object to what he thought was a fair number. Howard had promised him that he would support a fair housing allowance if he would stay at First Church and not go to Texas. He was beginning to feel betrayed. "Do you have a problem with the way that I arrived at this total? I mean, I did take the middle number each time. I determined it by basing everything on fair market value, the current mortgage rates, and an average of the last three years of actual expenses for the current Rectory."

Howard tried to appear sympathetic. "Misturh Austin, I certainly agree that you and the finance committee have put a lot of work into your endeavor. I'm grateful to all of you. I just think that we have to be realistic about how the congregation might respond. Remember, it's the members of the congregation that pay your salary. They're good people and they don't object to paying you a fair remuneration. But Misturh Austin, the number that you've proposed will be criticized. It's just unacceptable."

Elmer Idle could hardly sit still in his seat. He was frantically trying to seize on an opportunity to speak. "Father Austin, you need to know that your decision to sell our Rectory is not being well-received in this congregation. I don't know about the rest of the men at this table, but my phone has been ringing off the hook. I've had members of this congregation calling me in tears. They are, quite frankly, very concerned about what this Vestry is going to do about your request. I'm going to tell you something that no one else at this table appears willing to tell you, but this number that you've proposed for your housing allowance is nothing but sheer greed."

"Speak for yourself!" Stone, the Chief, and Henry all shouted at the same time. Several other members of the Vestry murmured their disagreement.

Elmer sat back in his seat. "That's my point. I'm not speaking for myself. I'm speaking for the majority of this congregation."

Stone Clemons made a chewing motion with his mouth. "Unless you're willing to give us the names of all those that you say you represent, I'm going to assume that you're speaking for no one but yourself."

"He's speaking for me!" Once again the voice of Ned Boone filled the room.

"Okay then." Stone nodded. "You're speaking for Ned Boone and yourself."

"Howard, if you don't find any problem with the process that Father Austin and the finance committee used to reach this number, then just what do you propose?"

"I'm pleased that you asked." Howard Dexter reached into a manila folder and began handing out sheets of paper. Steele immediately recognized them as the real estate flyers that Randi had shown him. "With all due respect to the Rector, he has failed to tell you that if he insists on selling the Rectory, the Altar Guild has selected three houses for him to choose from. They have gone to considerable labor to find a house that would be suitable for the Rector of First Church to live in.

Any one of these could be secured for considerably less than the housing allowance he has proposed. They could easily be funded from the sale of the Rectory and the excess funds from that sale could be placed in the endowment or the major repair fund for future repairs on the parish properties." It was difficult for Howard to hide the fact that he was very pleased with himself and his proposal. Of course, he also failed to acknowledge that the parish funds he was so anxious to embellish were deposited in his bank.

Henry Mudd looked through the flyers and then studied Steele's face. Steele was sitting quietly staring at the table. He was beginning to have second thoughts about San Antonio. He wondered if they had secured a Rector yet. He just knew that the three houses that the Altar Guild had chosen were unacceptable to Randi. He was not going to break her heart for this or any parish. He would resign before he'd do that. "Steele, have you and Randi seen these flyers?"

Steele nodded. "Yes, Mrs. Dexter and Mrs. Smythe gave them to Randi."

"And?"

Steele shook his head. "They're just not what we had in mind. Don't get me wrong. We really appreciate all that the Altar Guild did. They put a lot of work and effort into finding these three houses. I can also appreciate how Mister Dexter would like to take some of the funds from the sale of the Rectory and put them in the various endowments." Steele had to stop talking for a minute. His voice was beginning to break and tears were welling up in his eyes. He looked around the table. "Guys, I thought we had a deal. I turned down a very desirable call that would have allowed Randi to purchase the house of her choice. I was given the assurance that if I stayed at First Church, you would give me a housing allowance comparable to the fair market value of the current Rectory. That was the deal that I thought we had."

"I hope you're not questioning our integrity, Misturh Austin!" Howard Dexter was clearly agitated.

"No, sir, I don't mean any disrespect whatsoever. It's just that I thought we had a deal."

"Well, just what's wrong with these houses?" Howard Dexter glared at Steele. "These are all very nice houses. I would think any priest would be honored to live in one of these houses."

"They are just not what we have in mind."

"What's wrong with them?" Howard blasted.

"Nothing." Steele tried to keep his voice calm. "Nothing at all. They're very nice. It's just that we had wanted a new house with a modern kitchen, bathrooms and large closets. We had a new house in Oklahoma and Randi has missed all those things. We also wanted a house in a neighborhood of young families. We wanted to live where Travis and Amanda could have neighborhood playmates. Maybe even have playmates right next door. These three houses are in established neighborhoods. The residents are all older. There are no small children in these neighborhoods."

Howard was not about to relinquish his position. "I've heard that you've been looking at houses in Magnolia Plantation. That's clear out on the north side of town. A house in that location won't be convenient to our members for parish functions."

"No, sir, it wouldn't. I'd have to drive fifteen minutes to get to work. I realize that. But we're looking for a house and neighborhood for our children. We just want a home that is ours."

"Well, I can tell you right now that the parish won't like you living clear out there."

Steele grimaced. "I would hope that the parish would put my family and their needs before another building in which to host a parish social."

Henry Mudd had been thumbing through the file on the conference table in front of him. He handed Stone a copy of a document. "Stone, you're an attorney. Is it your legal opinion that this is a binding agreement?"

Stone smiled. "It is my legal opinion that any court in the land would uphold it as such."

Henry nodded. "That's my legal opinion as well. Howard, this is the agreement that we presented to Steele after we learned that he'd received the call to San Antonio. The work and the conclusions that Steele and the finance committee are presenting to us tonight are in keeping with that agreement. I fear that if we fail to honor it, Steele has substantial grounds for litigation against First Church. Is that your opinion, Stone?"

"He would win on the first go-around and we'd have no hope of having the decision overturned."

Henry handed the document to Howard. "Lest you have forgotten, Howard. This is your signature on the document. We have no recourse except to accept the recommendation of the finance committee. It's in that spirit that I make that motion."

Chief Sparks seconded and the motion once again passed with only Howard abstaining and Elmer voting against it. Ned Boone stood and stormed out of the conference room, slamming the door loudly behind him.

Steele was floating on air all the way home. He took the stairs two at a time. "Shh, Steele, you're going to wake the baby."

He took Randi in his arms and kissed her passionately. "What's gotten into you? You know that we can't do that just yet."

The smile on Steele's face started at his toes and washed over his entire body. "No, we can't do that, but tomorrow we can go pick out the house that we want."

Randi squealed. From the other room, Amanda let out a cry. The baby was now awake.

CHAPTER 22

"No one can stand her, Ned." Judith Idle's face was distorted with bitterness. "She prances around in her skin tight dresses showing off her size zero figure and her big...." She made a motion with her hands in front of her own chest. "She's just too much."

"Do all the women in the church feel that way?" Ned asked.

"Everyone I talk to does."

Ned, Judith, and Elmer were gathered for lunch at the Dogwood Café. It was a beautiful little café on a side street in the shadow of the First Church steeple. At one time it had been a little cottage home for a family. It had been converted into a café. There was a white picket fence around the property and a white wood archway over the entrance at the front sidewalk. The fence was covered with confederate jasmine. The archway was covered with wisteria blossoms that dropped like clumps of grapes through the trellis openings. Diners could eat in one of the small rooms throughout the house that had been remodeled into dining rooms. Or, if the weather was nice, they could sit at the tables on the front patio.

"Tell me more." Ned was hanging on to her every word. "What else do you hear about her?"

"Do you believe how fast she lost her baby weight?" Judith's eyes almost popped out of their sockets. "There are several of us that think she went to Atlanta and had some work done."

Elmer Idle chuckled. "You can't put anything past these women. They have a keen eye for these sorts of things. Personally, I don't think that a preacher should be married to a woman like her. I've heard several men right here in Falls City talk about her. I'm not one of them, because I'm devoted to this woman right here. But, I hear men talk. Quite a few of them think she's pretty sexy. I just don't think a preacher's wife should stir men up the way she does."

Now Judith Idle was perturbed. "Elmer, I can't believe you men. I never thought my husband would be involved in such a conversation."

"Now, calm down, Honey. I just overheard some guys talking in the locker room at the club. I wasn't a part of any such conversation."

"Oh, thank you, Jesus." Judith lifted her hands towards the heavens in an act of praise. She shut her eyes and prayed, "Sweet Jesus, thank you for giving me such a faithful and loving husband."

"What do you hear about their house hunting?" Ned frowned.

"I have a realtor friend that's been showing them houses out in Magnolia Plantation. Can you believe that? Elmer and I couldn't afford one of those houses. Now, the preacher and his blonde hussy are going to buy one of those fancy new houses. She just really thinks she's something with her handsome husband, two perfect little children and next a big house out in Magnolia Plantation. She just makes me sick."

"There's just something wrong with a preacher and his wife living in Magnolia Plantation," Elmer snorted.

"I agree." Ned nodded. "Howard Dexter and you did your best to help the Vestry deal with the consequences of such a decision, but it didn't do any good. Austin has loaded the Vestry with a bunch of his disciples. It just perturbs me to know that Henry Mudd and the Bishop appear to be in his camp now. He is a first-class con man. He's as slick as they come. This guy is really good. He's dangerous, I tell you. He's dangerous."

Judith Idle wasn't ready to give up on her critique of Randi. "Just how many women do you know that have a waist that small after giving birth? I think she has zero fat on her body. Have you noticed how she walks? She thinks she's some sort of a model. She strolls down the aisle of the church to the front pew like she's on a runway."

"From what I hear, the runway was in a strip club."

Judith and Elmer both shouted, "What?"

Ned nodded. "You heard me correctly."

Elmer smiled, "You sly fox. You've found out something. What have you discovered?"

Judith leaned forward across the table. She was only inches from Ned Boone's face. "I knew it. I knew she was a bit too good to be true. She acts like she's the perfect little preacher's wife. She tries to pretend to be the perfect mother. She's not fooling me. And she's not fooling the other women in the church. All the wives are complaining about how she flirts with their husbands. Now, what do you know?"

Ned chuckled, "Well, let's just say that our Rector's wife is anything but pure."

Elmer couldn't help but lick his lips. "Are you telling me she can be had?"

A broad, knowing smile spread across Ned Boone's face. "Let's just say that when I share with you what I know, you'll be shocked."

"Oh, I don't think so." Judith snickered. "I've had her figured out for some time. Her little purity act hasn't fooled me or most of the women in this church. I've had more than one conversation with other women in this town about her. We all think she's a phony. Personally, I think she's the typical slut turned preacher's wife."

"I agree with Judith, Ned. I don't think anyone is going to be that surprised. I've heard several men talk about how they thought she was coming on to them."

Judith gushed. "And I know several wives that are convinced that she was flirting with their husbands. Several wives have told me that she has actually kissed their husbands on their lips right in front of them. Now what do you think of that?"

Ned nodded. "What about Austin? Do you think he has any clue?"

"I don't think so." Elmer crossed his arms over his chest. "I've watched him. I think he's oblivious to her flirtations. He's a blind fool. He loves her and trusts her completely. When are you going to show us what you have?"

This time it was Ned Boone that folded his arms over his chest. He smiled broadly. "When the time is right, I plan to show everyone in this parish what I have on her. It won't take long until it's common knowledge in this entire city. Austin will be so humiliated he won't be able to get out of Falls City and away from First Church fast enough."

Once again, Judith lifted her hands in praise. "Thank you, Jesus. At last we'll be rid of that false prophet. Your Church will be saved." Then she began to chant quietly, "Thank you, Jesus. Thank you, Jesus," over and over again.

Ned Boone was amused by her piety. "Add to that prayer that they'll be no more of our hard earned money going to support queers and deadbeats. Our money will go to the real work of the Church."

"I'll add a big 'Amen' to that," Elmer chimed in.

The waiter came to their table and asked, "Are you ready to order?"

Ned Boone smiled. "Let's start with a bottle of your finest champagne. We have a lot to celebrate."

CHAPTER 23

Amanda was swallowed up by her baptismal gown. The antique white brocade cloth had originally been worn by Randi's great-grandmother as her wedding gown. The wedding gown was re-sized so that it could be her grandmother's baptismal gown. Randi's mother wore it at her baptism as did Randi. Now, little Amanda was wearing it for her baptism. The church was filled for the eleven o'clock Sunday morning service and baptism. Amanda was the only one being baptized.

Rob and Melanie had flown in from California. They would be Amanda's godparents. Both sets of grandparents had arrived and taken turns trying to make up for lost time with Travis. The entire baptismal party was seated on the front row of the church. Steele had given great thought to his sermon for the morning. "I've heard it said that spiritual people understand that our children are not our children. We understand that they are gifts to us from God. They came from God and one day they, like us, will return to God."

Steele looked down from the pulpit at his beautiful wife and children. "I suppose that there are many ways that a man and a woman might explain the mystery surrounding the birth of a child. For some, there is no mystery at all. The birth of a child is simply the merging of their DNA and a new biological creature comes into being. The distinctive nature of the new life is that it merely belongs to this particular species in the animal kingdom. There is no more of a mystery in the birth of a human than that of any other primate in the animal kingdom. It's just that our particular species over the passage of time has evolved and become more highly developed. So basically, for those who reduce the birth of a child to the merging of DNA, there is no mystery at all.

Spiritual people have a different understanding. For us, a child is not just the product of genetic material that, hopefully, will live out the predictable life cycle. We do not dismiss the miracle of a new human life as just another turn of the page in the cycle of evolution. For us a child is a unique part of God's creation. The birth of a baby transcends the scientific explanations of life. The Psalmist declared, *You formed my inward parts; You wove me in my mother's womb. I will give thanks to You, for I am fearfully and wonderfully made: Wonderful are Your works, And my soul knows it very well.* Our children are a manifestation of God's love for each of us. We refuse to explain them away with some scientific theory. We know them to be a miracle. When we look into the faces of our children, we also look into the face of God.

Our children are the product of two people's love for each other. They are an expression of our commitment to building a home and a family. Whether the children come into our lives through birth or adoption, they come to us because of the love that two people have for each other. It's a love that they want to share with another. We have made an intentional decision to share our lives with these little bundles of joy. We do this in spite of the fact that we fully realize that one day they will turn into a creature commonly known as a *teenager*." The congregation laughed and Steele smiled. "I apologize to all the teenagers that are here this morning. I especially apologize to those of you that I've just made uncomfortable. We're not laughing at you, we're laughing because all of us were once teenagers. We remember everything that you are thinking and feeling right now. I have often heard it said that the strictest fathers are simply men with good memories." Once again, there was laughter and the nodding of heads in the congregation.

"There is an old song that includes the words, *Every time I hear a new born baby cry, or touch a leaf, or see the sky—I believe.* Perhaps there are those that can hold a new life in their hands and reduce it to no more than a product of evolution. I confess that I'm unable to do so. Spiritual people throughout the millenniums have been unable to do so. Allow me to repeat what I said earlier, because these words so clearly distinguish spiritual people from those who are content to dismiss life as no more than a series of chemical reactions. A new life is not only an expression of two people's love for each other. A new life is also an expression of God's love for us. We have been granted the privilege of participating in God's creation process. We have become co-creators with the One that is the Creator of all things.

Now lest you think that I might over romanticize the little gifts of life, let me ground my words with a hard dose of reality. I fully realize that our children will also test us throughout their lives. There will be times of rebellion. There will be outbursts followed by slamming doors. I'm well aware that the words 'I hate you' may be hurled at us when we have to practice that thing called *tough love.* I remember my grandmother telling me that when children are small they walk on your feet and when they grow older they walk on your hearts. She told me about the woman that finally received a telephone call from her adult son. She said to him, 'Thank God that you finally called me. I haven't had a thing to eat for two weeks.' The son was shocked. 'Mother, why haven't you had anything to eat for two weeks?' Her response was classic. 'I didn't want to have my mouth full when you finally got around to calling me.' " Once again the congregation roared with knowing laughter.

"Our children will give us more than enough opportunity to practice unconditional love. You know, the kind of love that God has for us. Our sons and daughters will always be our sons and daughters. They will make us proud, but they will also disappoint. They will be obedient, but they will also rebel. They will be loving, but they will also be selfish. In short, they will live out the very human drama in their own lives that is preserved for all of us in the sacred book. But like God, we will continue to love them and love them and love them through it all."

Steele paused and looked out at the congregation. All were hanging onto his every word. Many of the parents and grandparents in the congregation were nodding their heads in agreement. He looked down at his own parents. His mother was holding Amanda. "My mother and father tell me that being a parent is the best thing that they ever did in their life. They now tell me that being a grandparent is God's way of rewarding them for being a parent." There were some very knowing chuckles throughout the congregation. "They promise me that being a grandparent is the best gift of all. As I've watched the complete adoration that Travis has poured on his grandparents these past few days, I'm now beginning to believe them when they tell me that the best is yet to be.

If we could keep our children locked up in our loving homes, perhaps life would be different for them. The reality is that we cannot. They will live out their lives in a confusing world. It's a world filled with choices, temptations, evil, and those who would, if given an opportunity, do them harm. The Evil One would gladly claim them for his own disciples and lead them down a path of self destruction. Left to their own devices, they would not understand that there is a better way. Baptism is the

Christian response to the dark realities of life and of this world. Here in this sacrament we acknowledge that these little lives have to be given the knowledge, the grace and the strength to make the right choices in life. Parents and godparents make sacred promises that they will do all in their power to teach the one being baptized by word and example.

You, the members of the congregation, make those same promises. Every household that presents a child for baptism is appealing to the household of God to assist them. In presenting Amanda for baptism, we're asking you to receive her into the larger Christian family. We're asking you to be a part of her life. We're asking that you be her family beyond our family. We're asking you to model for her the love of Christ. In the words of the prayer book, we are asking you to help us to teach her to *respect the dignity of every human being.*

For some in the world, a new life is simply the product of human biology. For Christians, baptism reminds us that a life is so much more. A child is a gift from God. The Bible reminds us that God knows each child by name. It teaches that God knows us each so intimately that He even knows the number of hairs we have on our heads. Because this Heavenly Father loves us so much, he instructs that we not be left to our own devices. Through Baptism, we become members of the Household of God. In the Household of God we are instructed, encouraged and nourished by Word and Sacrament on our spiritual journey. Baptism is acknowledging that our little bundle that is clothed in all that white damask this morning is not just the mingling of DNA. No, she and all children are the sons and daughters of God. Through Baptism we acknowledge that she belongs to God forever." Steele stopped and once again looked down at his little family. He smiled at Randi, who was now holding Amanda. "Jesus took the little children in his arms and blessed them. This is the moment when He will do the same for Amanda."

At the baptismal font, Steele had asked Horace to preside. Horace asked the baptismal questions and led the congregation in prayers. Steele stood next to Randi. Rob and Melanie stood with them. As the godmother, Melanie held Amanda in her arms. Steele's dad was holding Travis. The other grandparents proudly completed the baptismal party. When it came time to bless the water for baptism, Horace stood back so that Steele could bless the water in which to baptize his daughter. He then took Amanda from Melanie. He looked at Randi and forced a smile. His eyes were growing moist. Tears were streaming down her face. Steele's voice broke as he said to his wife, "Name this child." Randi's voice quivered as she answered. "Amanda Ellen."

Steele took the baptismal shell and poured the water over his daughter's head and baptized her. Amanda had been sleeping, but when the water washed over her forehead she let out a cry. He quickly wiped her forehead and calmed her down. To the congregation he said, "It's a good thing when the newly baptized cry. It just means that the devil is coming out of them." The congregation roared with laughter. Steele then took the oil of chrism and put some on his thumb. He made the sign of the cross on her forehead. "Amanda Ellen, you are sealed by the Holy Spirit in baptism and marked as Christ's own forever."

Steele then asked the congregation to receive the newly baptized. There was a thunderous round of applause. Then the choir and congregation started to sing, *we receive you into the Household of God.* The choir sang the words, *confess the faith of Christ crucified, proclaim his resurrection and share with us in his eternal priesthood.* Then the congregation would repeat over and over, *we receive you into the household of God.* Steele processed directly behind the crucifer and the two torchbearers as the baptismal party moved down the aisle from the baptismal font in the back of the church toward the front. Steele was carrying Amanda. Randi was walking next to him holding Travis' hand. The congregation continued to sing as they processed down the aisle, *we receive you into the household of God.*

When the procession was nearing the front of the church, Steele's heart suddenly skipped a beat. He looked to his left and saw Max and Sharon Weller smiling at him. Max and Sharon's daughter, Mandy, had died last year from a brain tumor. She was their only child. Steele stopped and did something he had never done before. He handed Amanda to Sharon. Sharon took Amanda in her arms. She continued to smile broadly as she mouthed the words, "She's beautiful" to Steele and Randi. Sharon then handed Amanda to her husband to hold. He kissed her on the forehead. Then, to Steele's surprise, Max handed her to Henry Mudd standing next to him. Henry held her for a minute. He started to hand her to his wife, Virginia, but she shook her head and sat down in the pew. So Henry handed Amanda to Almeda, who was sitting with Bud. They each held her for a moment and then continued to pass Amanda down the pew. Then his daughter was handed to the people in the pew in front of them. One by one the remaining members of the congregation held Amanda. All the time that she was being passed from person to person in the congregation they were singing, *we receive you into the household of God.* Finally, Amanda was given to the last person in the first pew. Steele took her and turned to face the congregation. The music stopped. He looked out at the congregation and in a loud clear voice he said, "Please greet your new sister in Christ Jesus." Once again the congregation exploded with applause. Steele handed Amanda to Randi and hugged them both. He then reached down and picked up Travis. Travis decided it was time to wave at the congregation. As he did, the congregation swelled with laughter and there was yet more applause.

CHAPTER 24

Rob and Steele decided to spend Monday on the golf course. Rob was convinced that he could get Steele excited about his new found passion for the game. Melanie and Randi wanted to take the opportunity to soak up some of the south Georgia sunshine. Steele's mother and father volunteered to take Travis and Amanda to the zoo. The two couples all went to the Magnolia Plantation Golf Club. This was a community club and golf course for residents and prospective residents of Magnolia Plantation. Steele had already made certain that there were no discrimination rules in the membership. While the men played golf, Melanie and Randi were able to sun at the community pool. When the guys finished their game they would all have an early dinner in the club dining room.

Randi decided to wear her new white bikini swimsuit. "You don't look like you ever had one child, let alone two." Melanie was admiring Randi. "Look at your legs. They're gorgeous."

"They need some sun on them." Randi smiled. "But thank you for the compliments. I had some second thoughts about wearing a bikini next to you since you have the perfect body."

"I don't think you have a thing to worry about."

"Do you and Rob plan on having any children?" Randi asked.

"We talk about it. Remember, he does have his one son. He's now in college at UCLA. I just love him, and he's really accepted me as Rob's wife. I think it was pretty hard for him at first. I had to assure him that I wasn't trying to replace his mother. I think we have a good relationship."

"So that's a definite maybe?"

"Oh, I don't know. Rob is a good fifteen years older than me so I don't know if he wants to start a second family."

"What about you?" Randi persisted. "What do you want?"

"I have to admit that holding Amanda and playing with Travis stirs my maternal instincts. Yes, I think I would like to have a baby with Rob.

Maybe I'm overly romantic, but I think having a baby with the man you love just sort of cements your souls together in a very special way. Do you think that's true?"

Randi stretched out on the lounge chair next to Melanie and pulled her sunglasses over her eyes. "When I watch Steele with the children...oh I don't know. He's just so gentle with them. Sometimes he gets down on the floor and plays with them like he's still five years old himself. And the way he looks at them. He's such a good daddy. Melanie, I never dreamed I could love him more than I already did. I can't explain it."

Melanie sat up and started rubbing suntan lotion on her arms and legs. "Oh, I think you just did. I want to feel that way too. Rob is a good father to his son, but he's older. I want to have a baby with him. I guess I just have to convince him."

Randi snickered, "Believe me Melanie, with that body I don't think you'll have any difficulty at all."

A waiter approached and asked if they wanted anything from the bar. They each ordered a diet drink. They continued to talk about their marriages, children, California, the Church, exercising, and dieting. All the time they continued to feel the warm sun wash over them. They were totally unaware that they were being watched by two men at the bar.

"Which one is the preacher's wife?" A young man sitting in short black swim trunks asked. His open shirt revealed a well developed chest and rippling stomach muscles. He was tan with bright blue eyes and coal black hair. His teeth were whiter than the clouds that hung lazily on the horizon. The muscles in his arms were accentuated by protruding blood vessels.

"She's the one in the white bikini."

"Who's the other one?"

"Oh, she's some rich girl from California that's married to an ex-priest that literally got away with murdering his own wife. He killed his wife so he could marry that whore."

"God, I think she's really hot. They're both hot. I want to do both of them."

"I want you to keep your eye on the job I've hired you to do. Your target is the preacher's wife. I'm not paying you for recreational diversions. Keep your mind on the task at hand."

The young man smiled. "It's a piece of cake. This is going to be so easy. I'm really going to enjoy this." He left the bar and walked toward the lounge chairs where Randi and Melanie were lying. He took his shirt off and tossed it on a nearby table. Randi was sitting up on the side of the chair squeezing some suntan lotion on her shoulders. The young man walked up behind her, "Here, let me help you with that." He took the tube from her and started rubbing the lotion on her shoulders and arms.

"Just a minute." Randi turned to look at him. "Just who are you?" She took the bottle of lotion from him.

He gave her a wide smile. His white teeth sparkled in the sunshine and his blue eyes glistened. "Oh, I'm the club's suntan man. They pay me to make sure that beautiful women apply plenty of lotion on their gorgeous bodies so that they don't get sunburned. I'm just doing my job."

Melanie was now sitting up looking at the young man over the top of her sunglasses. Randi glanced back at her. The two women started laughing. "Does that line really work for you?"

"What do you mean? That's not a line. It's my job." Then he sat down on the lounge chair directly behind Randi. At that moment she felt her bikini top go loose. She grabbed the front of it to hold it up.

"Did you do that?" She turned and gave him a stern look. "You must really be something to watch at a drive-in movie."

He held up his hands. "Honest, I didn't do anything. I just wanted to apply some lotion. You're beginning to turn red."

Randi stood. She was still holding the front of her bikini so that it wouldn't fall down. She pushed against his chest with her free hand. "Now you get out of here. You go some place else to do your job."

"Are you sure I can't help you?"

This time it was Melanie who sat all the way up. "You heard the lady. Now go find some little girls your own age to play with. Get out of here or I'm going to have you thrown out!"

The young man stood facing Randi. He took a long gaze in her eyes. He put his hands on her waist and jerked her up against his body. He brought his face close to hers as though he was going to kiss her. "Are you sure that's what you want?"

Once again Randi pushed against his chest. "I think you had better leave."

"Okay," he smiled. "I was just trying to help."

When he had gone Melanie asked, "Did you know that guy?"

Randi shook her head. "I've never seen him before. He was sort of cute though."

Melanie snickered. "The boy had a body on him didn't he?"

"He looked pretty good for a youngster, but I prefer a man."

Melanie pulled her sunglasses back over her face and stretched out on the lounge chair. "I don't guess we should tell Rob and Steele about this, should we?"

Randi decided that since her bikini bra strap was undone anyway she'd lie on her stomach and tan her back. She quipped back, "Oh, I don't think so. I've never really seen Steele jealous and I don't think I want to start now."

The young man strolled into the parking lot. He got into the back seat of a car. There were two men sitting in the front. The car drove out of the parking lot and onto the highway leading into town. "Well, how was that? Did you get some good pictures?"

The man in the passenger seat turned and handed the young man an envelope filled with cash. The young man quickly counted it. "This is more than we agreed to."

"That's because you did your job even better than I anticipated."

"Are you going to need me again?"

"We'll see how this goes. If I do need you, I know where to find you."

The driver of the car asked, "Do you want to go with me to my dark room to get these pictures developed?"

"I want those pictures developed and in my hands today. I'm going with you." And then, a big smile spread over Ned Boone's face.

CHAPTER 25

I don't care what that sorry excuse for a Bishop wants." John Collins was furious. "You go back and tell him exactly what he can do with his apology."

Robert Hayes gestured with his hands for John to calm down. "Father Collins…"

"Don't call me that!" He exploded.

"You're still a priest. I just wanted to show you the proper respect," Robert Hayes uttered, his voice little more than a whisper. All the visits he'd been making on the Bishop's behalf had taken a toll on him. Priest after priest had greeted him with bitterness and anger. He'd heard one heartbreaking story after another. He felt responsible for their suffering. While it had been the Bishop's doing, he'd stood back and not said anything. To the contrary, he'd actually helped bring each of these men and their families down. He had run out of energy. This was the last priest on the Bishop's list. He so wanted to reconcile with this man. It was his last chance.

"You and that purple-shirted fat boy are five years too late with your respect."

"Please listen to me, John. The Bishop is a changed man. He's had a couple of heart attacks and they've changed him. He really is a different man. He wants to make amends with all the priests that he feels like he's let down."

"I don't care if he's become a candidate for sainthood. The both of you sold me and my family down the river when we really needed your help. Now you're going to have to excuse me for a minute while I answer this phone call."

"I'd really like to talk with you just a bit more."

A disgusted look came over John's face. "I don't know what we have to talk about, but you can wait in the outer office."

The Chancellor took a seat in the waiting room outside John's office. It gave him some comfort to know that he was now the principal of a school.

Robert Hayes supported his forehead with his hand as he remembered the scenario that led to the priest's downfall. There was a small group in the parish in Savannah that wanted him removed. They had followed the pattern of so many others. First came the letters to the Bishop expressing *concerns for the parish*. The Chancellor had discerned that those determined to get rid of a priest always couched their grievances as *concerns for the parish*. The letters never contained complaints. They were always worded as *concerns*. Of course, the writers had the best interests of the parish at heart. They were appealing to the Bishop to take some action.

The letters of concern were then followed with those filled with suspicions about the priest. There were no accusations or evidence of wrongdoing, just suspicions. Sometimes they were around finances, sometimes they were about sexual improprieties, or not teaching the Bible, or personality problems. Occasionally, someone would write that they suspected the priest to have a drinking problem, or perhaps he was mentally ill. Rufus would show each letter to his Chancellor to keep him informed and protected legally. His response to them was always the same. He'd write the author and thank them for their concerns and their commitment to the parish, but he couldn't get involved without substantive evidence of wrongdoing.

The rumors of secret cottage meetings would come next. These were often followed by a visit from the priest to the Diocesan House. The Bishop would listen to the priest and suggest that he and the Vestry bring in a conflict management consultant. Depending on the parish and the size of their financial commitment to the Diocesan budget, Rufus would offer to meet with the two Wardens or the entire Vestry. Of course, he always wanted to do this without the priest being present so he could best mediate the situation. If he determined that the movement to remove the priest was being led by the wealthier patriarchs of the parish, then he chose his favorite course of action. He would do nothing. When the patriarchs were in support of the priest and the movement was being led by a small group of antagonists, Rufus still took his clue from the patriarchs. If they weren't willing to come to the priest's aid, then neither was he. It would just be a matter of time until the priest would get so tired of the fight that he would leave of his own accord. The group that went after Father John Collins had been particularly relentless. Their attacks had been vicious. John appealed to Rufus to intervene on several occasions. He assured John that he would have a word with the antagonists. He never did.

"I only have a few minutes left before my next appointment." John Collins invited the Chancellor back into his office.

"I know that you must be busy and I do thank you for seeing me, but I want you to think about the significance of this gesture. The Bishop has paid for me to fly all the way out here to Arkansas to apologize to you. He wants to try to help you get another parish. He wants to encourage you to begin an active parish ministry again."

"Then why isn't he here himself?"

"Like I said, he's had two heart attacks. He simply isn't well enough yet to travel, so he sent me. Believe me, his intentions are sincere. His heart is in the right place."

John Collins leaned back in his chair and studied the Chancellor's face. "As I said before, he's too late. He threw me to the wolves. Ninety-eight percent of the people in that parish supported me in my ministry. There were only a half dozen or so malcontents that went after me. They wanted me to be *their boy* and I refused. The Bishop left me to end my ministry there under a veil of innuendo and suspicion. He did absolutely nothing to correct that either. In fact, he made things worse. He actually wrote a letter to the parish leaders stating that he knew that I'd had an extramarital affair in my former parish. Now, Mister Hayes, you and I both know that it wasn't true. It was slander. Do you remember that letter? It was the final straw."

Tears welled up in Robert's eyes. He nodded. He also recalled just how jealous Rufus had been of this particular priest's popularity and success. "I remember. I know all that you're saying is true, but the Bishop wants to make amends."

John started to end the meeting and then had a second thought. "There's something I want that Bishop to know. I want you to go back and tell him what that experience did to me and my family. We got out of there under a cloud of shame that was not our doing. The six months severance didn't last because my entire family had to go to a psychiatrist to be treated for post-traumatic stress syndrome. My daughter suffered nightmares for months about how the mean church people were coming to get her daddy. At a hundred dollars an hour two and three times a week, we went through our money very quickly. The only job I could find was in a hardware store. Think about that. I went from preaching the Gospel and celebrating Mass to selling paint. My wife had to work in a fast food restaurant. We were all so depressed and anxious that we were on pills to put us to bed at night and still other pills to calm us down in the daytime. As for the Church, we want nothing to do with it. We all still believe in God, but we want nothing to do with the Church. As for me being a parish priest again, no, thank you. I'm now the principal of a school and we're getting our lives back together. Tell that Bishop that I can find more genuine Christian love in a strip club than there is in him or the Church. Now, please leave. I really don't want to hear anything else you have to say."

Robert Hayes stood and nodded. "Will you accept my apology? I'm genuinely sorry."

John Collins walked quickly from behind his desk and opened the door. "You're an attorney, right?"

"Yes."

"Well, attorney, if you don't get off this school property in the next five minutes, I'm going to have my security guards remove you. Is that a sufficient answer to just what you can do with your apology?"

Robert Hayes turned and walked out of the office directly to his rental car. This was the eighth priest he had tried to apologize to on behalf of the Bishop and himself. He had heard all their stories. He had heard the pain and turmoil that the Church had brought on them and their families. Six of the priests had come out of their vilifications with new and better financial circumstances than they would have ever had in the Church. Two of the priests had not done as well. Both of their marriages had ended in divorce. Both were now working at menial jobs. He suspected that both were either drinking heavily or sedating themselves with prescription medicines. Both were living in one-room apartments. They were a pitiful sight to behold. None of the eight or their families wanted anything else to do with the Church. They were lost from it forever.

He sat thinking about how the Church and the Bishop he loved had failed these good people. He thought about all the things he could have done or said to intervene. He thought about how he had also let these men and their families down. There were so many things he could have said to the Bishop to encourage him to come to the aid of those priests.

Now it was too late. The damage to all those men and their families had been done. It was now beyond repair. They had been called by God to be priests. Their only mistake was serving a congregation in Rufus Petersen's Diocese. He thought about the pain and humiliation that not only the clergy had suffered, but their wives and their children. While each story and been different, they were still all the same. He shuddered as he recalled the horror stories that the wives and children had lived through. More often than not it wasn't what the Bishop had done, but what he'd failed to do.

He laid his head on the steering wheel of his rental car and closed his eyes. He could handle no more. He simply couldn't listen to another heartbreaking story. He knew that he would not be able to absorb any more of the anger that these men and their families had for him. Their pain had become his pain. It was unbearable. The remorse in his heart over the way he and the Bishop had allowed a handful of people in each parish to destroy these priests and their families was overwhelming. The tears rolled down his cheeks. His body shook with grief for these good men called and anointed by Jesus. He reached into the glove compartment. He took out a box and opened it. He removed the contents. He quickly put it to his temple and pulled the trigger.

CHAPTER 26

Thank you so much for having lunch with me."

"Please, there's no need to thank me."

"You and Henry are so special to both Elmer and me. We have always admired the two of you. You're both such fine examples for all the people in our parish."

Virginia Mudd glanced away. "Thank you."

"Elmer and I still talk about that wonderful luncheon you hosted for Bishop Petersen. Virginia, there's just not a woman in all of Falls City that can hold a candle to your dinner parties. Everything was done with such class and good taste. Your party really was the talk of the town for weeks."

Virginia forced a smile. "You're much too kind."

"Nonsense, you and I both have suffered through social occasions that simply were not planned well."

"Yes, I suppose that's true."

"I do have to admit that I didn't get much of an opportunity to talk to one of your guests. I do remember correctly, don't I? Wasn't that Museum Director, Jacque Chappelle at your party?"

"Yes," Virginia answered weakly.

"Oh, I'm so sorry." Judith Idle put her hand over her mouth. "Silly me, that's got to be embarrassing for you. But of course you didn't know anything about his adulterous relationship with a married woman at the time, did you?

Virginia shook her head.

"I do apologize. It's got to be embarrassing for you to have had that piece of scum in your home as an honored guest just weeks before his sins were exposed to the entire community."

Again, Virginia shrugged.

"Do you have any idea just who the woman was? Everyone in town has been trying to figure it out. There's lots of speculation. I can just imagine that she must live in terror that her husband will find out. Can you imagine just how awful it's going to be for her when she's exposed? She'll be the talk of the town. I don't see how she'll be able to show her self anywhere." Judith sat up straight and a devious smile crossed her face. "The Bible reminds us that the sinners will have to pay for their sins. When it all comes out, and you know it will, she's going to get exactly what she deserves. Don't you think that adulterers should be punished for their sins?"

Virginia took a sip of her glass of wine so that she didn't have to answer. The waitress arrived and asked if they were ready to order their lunches. They each placed their order. Virginia took a big swallow of her wine. She needed all the courage she could muster. "Judith, I asked you to have lunch with me because I think I'm in need of a spiritual director."

"Oh, God bless you, Virginia. Elmer and I were talking about you just the other night. We were doing our evening devotions together. We end each day with Bible study and prayer. Anyway, we have been worried that Henry's not acting right. He seems to have become awfully close to Steele Austin. So we just lifted both of you up in prayer. I do hope you felt God's presence as we prayed for you. It's really none of my business, and you'd know best since you're his wife, but don't you think that Henry has changed?"

Virginia nodded. "Yes, he has."

Judith's eyes widened. "And you don't agree with him on that, do you?"

"No. Not really."

"We were afraid of something like this. That Steele Austin is so slick. He really is the devil incarnate. We women, however, have a sixth sense about these things. We can see right through his charade. Have you tried to talk to Henry about the Rector?"

"Not really."

"It probably wouldn't do any good. Have you heard that the Rector has bought a house in Magnolia Plantation?"

"I heard something about it."

"Can you believe it? None of the houses the Altar Guild went to all the work to find for him were acceptable. He had to go all the way out to the affluent north side to buy a house. It's just all so disgusting. What do you think of his wife?"

"I haven't cared much for her from the day they arrived. I really don't think she's a true blonde."

"Oh, I don't either. She just thinks she's so great. Now that she has a big house in Magnolia Plantation, I just think she's going to be intolerable. I really wish someone would bring the both of them down a notch or two. They really need to be put in their place."

"Judith, I wanted to talk to you about marriage. You and Elmer have such a perfect marriage. I was hoping that I might be able to learn a few things from you."

Judith reached across the table and took Virginia's hand. "Of course, I should have seen it. Your differences over the Rector are putting a strain on your and Henry's marriage. I'm so sorry. There's just no end to that man's destructive powers."

Tears welled up in Virginia's eyes. "Judith, I'm afraid that I'm going to lose my husband. I feel like he's pulling away from me. We're just not as close as we once were."

"Has anything happened?"

Virginia dabbed at her eyes. "No."

Judith's eyes grew wide. "Virginia, I don't mean to upset you, but usually when a man starts to pull away, it's a sign that there's someone else. Do you suspect that he's involved with another woman?"

Virginia shook her head. "No, it just feels like he doesn't want to be married to me. He's so distant."

"Hmmm, that is suspicious. And you're sure that there are no signs of another woman? I've noticed that he's losing weight. That's usually a dead giveaway. Is he going to the gym more than usual? Has he updated his wardrobe? Are you getting hang-up phone calls?"

"No, he's just lost some weight he needed to lose. Doctor's orders, you know."

"Well, then it could be that...no, that's probably not it either."

"What?"

"Do you think he's a homosexual?"

For the first time in weeks, Virginia started laughing. "No, no, a thousand times no. If there's one thing I'm absolutely sure of, it's that Henry is not gay." Virginia smiled. "Judith, I came to you for spiritual guidance. If your husband were pulling away from you, what would you do? That's what I want you to tell me."

Judith studied Virginia's face. "Well, I would start with the scriptures. I'll write down all the passages having to do with marriage. The Bible is full of counsel for wives. There are some very explicit instructions on just how a wife is to conduct herself. Of course, being chaste in the marriage is a given, but then you don't have to worry about that. Beyond that, a wife is to respect her husband and to love him completely. Oh, I'll just write down all the verses and you can memorize them for yourself. I just can't help but believe that you're already doing all of them."

"What else?"

"Prayer, Virginia. You must pray continually for your husband and for your marriage. And pray constantly for yourself. Pray that you'll be a wife that is worthy of Henry's love. Pray that the Holy Spirit will guide your every word and every action. Pray that God will nudge you to do those things that a godly wife may forget to do from time to time."

Virginia listened carefully. "That all sounds good."

"Well, it may be as simple as that." Just then their luncheon entrees arrived. When the waitress had refilled Judith's glass with sweet tea and Virginia's wine glass, she walked away. Judith Idle leaned across the table. She looked around and then whispered, "What about the sex?"

Virginia didn't anticipate that question and almost choked on the big gulp of wine she had just swallowed. "Why Judith, you really don't expect me to answer that?"

Judith giggled. "If I'm going to be your spiritual director I've got to know everything."

"What is it you want to know?"

"Judith, a husband has to feel like his wife really desires him. He needs to know that she thinks he is…well, you know, sexy. One of the quickest ways to kill a marriage is for a man to no longer feel like his wife wants him in that way. You know, men are like women in that sense. If he doesn't feel like you want him, then he begins to look for someone who does. Of course, if he begins to think that you would really rather be making love to someone else and not to him in that way, then it's all over." Judith smiled, "But Henry doesn't have anything to worry about in that area with you."

Virginia felt the tears welling up in her eyes. She didn't want to cry in front of Judith. She excused herself to go to the restroom. When she returned she had gotten herself under control. "Judith, I didn't mean for you to wait on me. You should have started eating."

"Oh, I never eat without praying first. Let me pray with you." Virginia took her seat again and Judith took both of Virginia's hands in hers. "Oh, sweet Jesus, you are so good to us. You have given us both such wonderful husbands. They are good men, pure in virtue. Their integrity is beyond question as is their love for us. Just as you blessed the Wedding at Cana with your presence we ask you to bless our marriages. I especially lift up Henry and Virginia and ask that you bless their marriage. Give Virginia the wisdom to be the kind of wife that Henry will always be able to love openly and completely. Let her faithfulness to him be a treasure beyond price. Work your miracles in their marriage so that from this day forward he will rise up and call her blessed." Then Judith began to whisper over and over again, "Thank you, Jesus. Thank you, Jesus. Thank you, Jesus."

As Virginia was driving home she was filled with disappointment. She had hoped that Judith might have been able to help her. She hadn't. Her piety had only made her feel more guilty than ever.

CHAPTER 27

The word spread quickly around the Diocese that the Bishop would not be presiding at or even attending the funeral of his long-time friend, Robert Hayes. Most of the clergy of the Diocese were relieved. They really didn't want to go either. Rufus Petersen and Robert Hayes had been a duo that few, if any, had been able to cross. Any priest that was silly enough to go up against them was certain to lose. Needless to say, the grief over the Chancellor's passing in the Diocese was limited to the immediate family. Rufus Petersen was perhaps the lone grieving person in the entire state that did not share some DNA with the now departed Robert Hayes.

When the Bishop received the news that his best friend had taken his own life in a rental car parked in a school parking lot in Arkansas, he collapsed. Once again his loyal secretary called 911 and he was rushed to the nearest emergency room. While there was no medical explanation for his collapse beyond the shock of the news, his cardiologist instructed that he not subject himself to the stress of a funeral service. The Bishop from the neighboring Diocese of Florida drove to Savannah to preside at the service.

Steele and Horace rode to Savannah together to be in attendance. Beyond the family, there was just a sprinkling of mourners. Steele and Horace made up two of only a half dozen clerical collars in the Cathedral. The service consisted of the Burial Office and nothing more. There was some organ music, but no hymns were sung. The reading of the three lessons and a Psalm made up the bulk of the liturgy. There was no obituary read, no eulogy, and no sermon. The total service from start to finish lasted less than fifteen minutes. The interment was in the Cathedral Cemetery. It too was brief and to the point. If there was to be an after-funeral reception, it was not announced. Horace and Steele returned to Falls City.

Steele had just settled back in his office when one of the matriarchs of the parish appeared at his open door. She was a large woman wearing a bright yellow sweater that made her appear all the wider. She was wearing the ever so predictable set of pearls around her neck and a gold broche in the shape of the State of Georgia. She was leaning on a brass and polished wood walking cane. Steele immediately concluded that the cane was more decorative than functional. "Misturh Austin, I simply must have a word with you."

From the day that he had arrived, Steele had learned that there were certain names in the parish that he could struggle to remember. He also learned that there were the names of another group of people that he had better never forget. She was at the top of the list of the second group. "Mrs. Horry, please do come in. I've just returned from the funeral for the Chancellor of the Diocese in Savannah."

She began to hobble toward him, leaning heavily on her cane. She shook her head, "Tragic, such a waste. One can only wonder what would possess such a holy man to take his own life." She took a seat next to Steele's desk. Once seated, she appeared to be studying Steele for several minutes as though she were taking a mental photograph of him before sketching his picture. "You're much more handsome from a distance."

Steele blushed. He wasn't sure how to respond to her comment. He stuttered, "I guess all our imperfections are more visible when we are seen close up."

She continued to stare at him. Steele was becoming uncomfortable under her gaze. "Yes, I suppose that's true."

"On the positive side, you don't appear to be nearly has heavy without your robes. Those robes make you appear to be much heavier."

Steele's discomfort under her icy stare and now her critique caused him to shift in his seat like a schoolboy just caught misbehaving. "Gosh, I was hoping the robes would do a better job of hiding all my imperfections."

"Well, they don't." She murmured. "I see I'm making you uncomfortable." Then she started looking around his office. "I don't believe I've been in here since you took up residence."

"Some would say that's a good thing."

She nodded, "I suppose so. I suppose so."

She took another long look at Steele. Once again he felt like she was about to take out a sketch pad and start drawing him. "Now tell me, how do you like our fair city?"

"Actually, Randi and I have just bought a house here. Falls City is beginning to feel like home."

"Yes, yes indeed." She wrinkled her nose. "Now, tell me. Why would you want to buy a house clear out on the north side of town? It's so far from everybody."

"We thought long and hard about where we wanted to settle. There are a lot of young families in that neighborhood. There will be children for our children to play with. The public schools are excellent out there. And while it sounds far away it really is only a fifteen minute drive."

Once again she studied him. "You say the public schools are excellent. I assumed you would send your children to the parish school."

"We're going to wait to decide that later."

"You can wait all you want, but I just don't think it will sit well with this parish if the Rector were to fail to send his children to his own school."

"I understand. It's something to consider."

Again there was silence as she slowly looked around Steele's office as though she were trying to remember every detail. He knew that she was a very precise person socially and educationally. There was a street named after her family in Falls City and one building at the local college. He knew that she was a fourth or fifth generation Georgian. She was a widow with no children. Her only heir was a niece living in Atlanta. Steele had been told that First Church was included in the distribution of her final estate for a considerable amount of money. But she had also included the college, hospital, and several other charitable endeavors throughout the state. While her fortune was supposed to be immense, her annual pledge to the parish did not reflect the same.

"Misturh Austin, it's just a bit of an irony that you've been in attendance at a funeral service this very day. I'm here to discuss my own funeral plans with you."

"I'm sorry, Mrs. Horry. Are you ill?"

"Oh, there's nothing to be sorry about. I'm quite well, thank you. I'm approaching the age when one does not want to leave these matters to chance."

"Well, I'm glad to hear that."

"If all goes well, you will not even be in attendance at my service, nor will the next Rector. I should hope to live to well past one hundred, but just in case I do not, I want my wishes on file here at the church. You do have a safe place for keeping these sorts of things, don't you? I would assume you keep them in the parish vault."

"Actually, they're kept in a secure fireproof safe right here in my office. It's where all the historic documents are kept as well as trusts, copies of final wills, and the wishes of those who have pre-planned their final services."

"Well, that's all very comforting."

"Now you need to know that I was at the funeral home earlier today. I have already chosen my casket and burial fault. My family monument is positioned here in First Church Cemetery. I'll be buried next to my husband. The only thing that will need to be added to our monument is the date of my departure."

"Go on."

"Now at the funeral home my search for a suitable casket in which to rest was just a bit disappointing. I wanted something with a yellow interior. As you can see, I like to wear yellow. My late husband said that I was most beautiful in yellow. So when I see him again I want to be wearing yellow. I also want to look my best for the many mourners who will want to come to the funeral home to view my body and pay their final respects."

Steele struggled not to laugh. "Were you successful in your quest?"

"Actually not, it was all so frustrating. They had all shades of blue, white, grey, pink…why they even had a casket lined with red cloth out there, but not a single one in yellow. I was a bit surprised to see that they had caskets for graduates of the University of Georgia, Georgia Tech, and Auburn." She shook her head. "But they did not have a single yellow casket."

"So what did you decide?"

"Well, I ended up choosing the exterior only. Mister Chisholm, the funeral director out there, now that's Mister Harry L. Chisholm, the father…not Gerald Chisholm. That's the son. I only wanted to deal with the father. That funeral home has been in his family for six generations. Now Gerald, when his father passes, will mark the seventh generation. Anyway, Mister Chisholm assured me that if I would simply bring him a bolt of yellow silk cloth he could have the casket of my choosing lined with it in one day. So that's what I've done."

"And you're going to be buried in a yellow dress."

"That's right. A yellow dress in a yellow casket...I told you, I wanted to be wearing yellow when I see my husband."

Steele tried his best not to conjure up the image of this massive woman wearing a yellow dress lying in a yellow lined casket, but to no avail.

"Now there are several other things that I have written out here in my instructions that I simply insist must be honored. First, any flowers sent to the funeral home or church are to be given to the patients in the hospital. I have gone down to Albert Rawlings and left written instructions for two large bouquets of yellow roses that are to stand at the head and foot of my casket. They will be of a large enough composition that no other flowers will be needed. I am leaving these same instructions regarding flowers for the Altar Guild. Two large bouquets of yellow roses are to be on the altar for my service. No other flowers are to be allowed or needed. There will also be plenty of fresh yellow flowers of all kinds delivered by Albert Rawlins to the cemetery. There will be no need to bring the ones from the funeral home or the church altar. I think that's so tacky anyway. I prefer that the flowers be fresh. I especially do not want any flower arrangements at the graveside that I've not previously approved. Some of the florists in this town just go overboard and they are not in good taste at all. I've personally selected the design with Albert for each bouquet that will be at my gravesite. You can always trust him to exercise excellent taste."

Steele was struggling not to have his mind clouded with all the yellow that would be surrounding this woman's burial. "Is there anything else?"

"Oh, for goodness sakes, yes; I have it all written down here for you, but I want to go over every detail. Now as for my funeral, I do expect that there will be a very large congregation of mourners, so I've enclosed a seating chart." The woman opened a large architect's rendering of the interior of First Church for Steele to look at. Every pew had handwritten notations on it. "The governor, our two senators and our congressman will sit on the same pew with my niece. Their wives will sit immediately behind them. Then I have left instructions for the seating of the various state and city dignitaries. Since I have no way of knowing what their names will be thirty or forty years from now, I've simply listed their seating places by office. As you can see for yourself, the various elected officials will fill the church and both transepts. I've left the balcony open for those not holding tickets for assigned seats."

"You've really gone to a lot of work."

She smiled at him. "I suppose so, but one's funeral is something that needs to be well-planned."

Steele smiled and nodded. He realized she was quite serious about all this.

"As for music, I do want a small string ensemble from the college to play. I have already chosen the music. It's listed here. You'll notice that I've left particular instruction that under no circumstances is that hymn, *Amazing Grace,* to be played. It's simply not Episcopalian. I just don't understand why everyone wants that awful tune played at their funerals. It sounds just like an Irish Pub Song."

"You realize that *Amazing Grace* was written by an Episcopalian and it's in our hymnal?"

"Misturh Austin, please do not presume to instruct me on music. I have my degree in music and I know of that which I speak. That hymn was written by a Methodist slave trader. The Methodists are nothing more than social climbers with a little religion thrown in for good measure. Now are my instructions clear on this one?"

Steele decided not to challenge her further. "If everything is written down, I'm quite sure the priest in charge of your service will honor your requests."

"Speaking of that...I have left instructions that the Bishop of the Diocese preside at my service. If he's unavailable than the Bishop of Atlanta or the Bishop of Alabama, in that order, are to be summoned. It's important that you understand that my family has always been closely associated with the Bishops of the Church. A Bishop presided at my parents' burial and their parents' burial. A Bishop has presided at every one of my family members' burials for well over a hundred years. A Bishop will preside at mine as well."

Steele nodded, "Yes, ma'am."

"Now the rest of this really doesn't concern you, it has to do with the reception following my funeral. It too will be by invitation. My house staff will be instructed to send any and all gifts of food to that Soup Kitchen you opened. It is still in operation isn't it?"

"Yes."

"Well, good. Do you think it'll still be in operation in thirty or forty years?"

"Gosh, I don't have any way of knowing, but unless we can do something to alleviate poverty and homelessness in this city, I should imagine it will still be needed."

"Well, I can only hope that it will be open. I just don't know what we'll do with all the food that the community will be sending over to my house if it isn't. I do suppose there's always going to be people looking for a handout. They should be happy to get all the casseroles that my friends will be sending over."

A feeling of disbelief at what he was hearing began to wash over Steele. "If you say so."

"I do. The affair following my funeral will be catered. True to the southern tradition of fine entertainment, there will only be sliced meats available at several carving stations. Fresh fruits and vegetables will be available on silver serving trays. I will have several bars attended by well trained bartenders both in my house and in the tent behind it."

Steele wrinkled his forehead, "A tent?"

"Yes, a tent. I do have a large home, but I will not be able to get all the invited guests into my house. I have left instructions that a large tent be placed behind my house to accommodate the overflow, but all that is none of your concern. My business manager will see to it."

"Yes, of course."

"Now there's one more thing about the menu that I simply insist the caterer honor."

Steele was about to remind her that in her own words the menu was not his concern, but his curiosity was getting the best of him. "Go on."

"Dessert will be key lime pie, but it will be real southern-style key lime pie. Can you believe I was at a luncheon just the other day and they served green key lime pie? It was as green as the leaves on that tree outside your window. It was on a dark chocolate cookie crust. I guess they'd made it out of Oreo cookies or some such nonsense. And then can you believe they put chocolate chips on top of it? Now mind you, that's Yankee pie! That's not the way we southerners make our key lime pies. I've also made it clear I don't want the key lime pie they make down there in Florida either. "

"I'm sorry. I fear that I don't know anything about the key lime pies they make in Florida."

She wrinkled her nose in disgust. "They use graham crackers to make the crust. That's just unforgivable. No, we'll have a real flour crust. That's the way we true southerners make our key lime pies."

Steele was glad he had allowed her to continue. "Is there anything else?"

She shifted in her seat just a bit. "Well, there is something I suppose I should tell you. She pointed to the seating chart she had previously opened on Steele's desk. "You see this spot right next to the Governor on the front pew."

"Yes, the one marked with a question mark."

"Yes, that's the one. That spot is reserved for my associate, if he should survive me."

Steele was really confused. "Your business associate?"

She chuckled, "You really are an innocent one, aren't you? No, Misturh Austin, he's not my business associate. He's my associate."

"Your associate?"

"Do I have to spell it out for you? We southern women have our pearls, our class, a little bit of sass, and we lucky ones have an associate."

She must have seen the blank look on Steele's face. He decided to try one more time. "I'm really sorry. I just don't understand."

"He's my gentleman friend, Mister Austin. Socially prominent women such as myself who are fortunate enough to have a special male friend in their lives refer to them as their associates. Now do you understand?"

Steele nodded, "I think I do now. Thanks for the explanation."

"Well, now that we've gotten through that, there's just one more part of my instructions I want to make crystal clear."

"Yes."

My business manager will have my social secretary write all the acknowledgements for the many gifts of flowers, food, and charitable contributions that will be made in my memory. I have left specific instructions that these not be written on those notes that the funeral home provides. I have already placed an order for especially designed and printed thank-you notes from the Crane Stationery Company for this purpose. Of course, they won't be actually printed and shipped until my time has come."

Steele's head was now swimming with all the details. "Well, it sounds like it's going to be quite a funeral."

"Mister Austin, my funeral will be the social event of the season. People will be talking about it for years after. It's just a shame that you're going to miss it." She handed him the folder. "Now, you put this is your safe. I've also given copies to my business manager, my attorney, my secretary, my niece, and the funeral director. My wishes will be honored." She stood and started walking toward the door. "Well, thank you for your time. You have a nice office. I hope you don't come to regret buying that house out on the north side."

"I think we'll be just fine. I'll put your file in my safe."

She turned and looked back, "One more thing I need to emphasize. There will be no preaching at my funeral! I've already written out a eulogy summarizing my family's genealogy, my many educational and social accomplishments, as well as my multitude of charitable endeavors. That is to be read in its entirety without any editing or editorial comment. Understood?"

"Understood," he smiled. She continued to hobble out the door. He stood and watched her as she progressed down the hall. Then he thought, every now and then there's a funeral he'd really like to preach. Hers was one of them.

CHAPTER 28

"What's this?"

The detective had tossed a folded newspaper on Henry's desk. Then he laid a stack of cash on top of it. "We won't be needing this."

Henry shot him a confused look. "What do you mean?"

"It's all right there for you to read. It's on the front page of that newspaper. I think you'll recognize one of the pictures." The detective sat down with an amused look on his face.

Henry opened the paper. There was a picture of a bloody bed in a hotel room. Then there were three pictures. Henry immediately recognized one of the headshots. It was Jacque Chappelle. The headline read, "Husband catches wife in love nest. Kills One, Critically Wounds the Other." He looked back at the detective.

"It seems that the husband was way ahead of us. He already suspected his wife. We never even gave him the pictures we had taken. He had his own detectives following her. He caught the two of them in the act. He blew a hole through his wife's heart with a shotgun. He put the gun between Chappelle's legs and surgically removed his external apparatus. He's in critical condition in the Raleigh hospital. I checked on him. They think he's going to recover, but he'll be conducting all necessary business through a plastic tube for the rest of his life."

"What about the husband?"

"Oh, they arrested him, but he's hired Duke Monahan to defend him."

"You mean the hot-shot lawyer that got that movie star off for shooting his wife?"

The detective laughed. "Yeah, he's the one. He's really, really good and really, really expensive, but he got that movie star off. He pled temporary insanity. He made the case that any loving husband would go crazy if he caught his wife in the act with another man. He had nine married men on his jury and three married women. He won his case. The husband walked free."

"Has the husband set up a defense fund? I'd like to contribute."

"I don't think he needs a defense fund. Remember, he's the C.E.O. of a big insurance company. I think he has plenty of money for his defense, but I'll check on it."

Henry sat silent for a few minutes. "You know I've finally figured out why an adulterous wife was taken out into the town square and stoned to death in Jesus' time."

"Oh?"

Henry nodded. "It was the only way that the husband could be put out of his pain and misery. If she wasn't around to remind him of her betrayal he could move on with his life. As long as he had to look at her, he was reminded of what she'd done. His hurt would be unending."

"Well, the laws don't allow that anymore."

"Maybe not, but this man has done what every betrayed husband in the same situation thinks about doing. At the very least, he put one French predator out of commission. He'll spend the rest of his life regretting violating other men's wives. I'm a New Testament Christian, but damn, this just seems like the right way to handle these situations. Do you mind if I keep this newspaper?"

"No, what do you plan to do with it?"

"Oh, I think I'll just leave it in the middle of my wife's bed. I really think she should read it."

"Do you want us to continue to keep an eye on her?"

"Oh, I don't know. Since this frog is out of commission I'm not sure it's necessary."

"So that's a no?"

Henry shook his head. "I'll tell you what. Follow her for the rest of the month. Let's see what she's up to and then we'll decide."

"You want me to continue the wire taps and all?"

"Yeah, let's just continue the full surveillance on her until the end of the month. Then come back and see me."

The detective left and Henry leaned back in his chair and read the article. He read it again. And then he read it again. He smiled. He really wasn't a vengeful man. But somehow or other the thought of the frog having to relieve himself through a plastic tube for the rest of his life brought him a lot of satisfaction.

"What are you smiling about?"

Henry looked up to see Dee, his new receptionist standing at his desk. "Oh, I just received some really good news. I was reading about it here in the newspaper."

Dee leaned forward to hand Henry his messages. When she did her full bosom poured out over her low cut dress. Henry's eyes were automatically drawn to the beauty that nature had spread before him. She saw his gaze and smiled. He smiled back at her. She handed him his messages. Her hand grazed his as he took them from her. He felt a tingle run up his spine. "You know that you promised to take me to lunch to welcome me to your office." She smiled at him again and stood back from his desk so that he could get a full view. She was wearing a tight little sun dress that accented her small waist. Her long legs were beautifully set in her high heels.

Henry took in the entire picture. She was a beautiful woman and he liked looking at her. "Do you have luncheon plans for today?"

"It's a little early to go to lunch right now, don't you think? It's not even ten o'clock yet." She smiled a teasing smile at him.

"I didn't mean right now." He smiled back. "I was thinking about lunch time."

"I'd be honored, Mister Mudd. I'll punch out at twelve noon sharp. Will that work for you?"

"Twelve noon it is."

She turned and walked away. At the door she turned her head to look back at him. She gave him a warm smile. "I can hardly wait."

Henry had lots to do. He had a big case he was getting ready for trial. But for the next two hours he was unable to concentrate. He could still feel her hand graze against his. He thought of her smile. He remembered her bosoms pouring over her sun dress. He thought of her long legs and her tiny waist. He finally just shut the files on his desk and watched the clock. He was feeling things he was beginning to think he'd never feel again. At eleven forty-five, he realized he could stand it no longer. He walked out to the front office. "It would work best for my schedule if we could go now."

She stood and brushed against him. He felt her breasts slide across his chest. She smiled at him. He got a whiff of her perfume. Her smell was intoxicating. "You're the boss. Just give me a minute to put the answering service on notice."

Henry Mudd felt like a teenage boy. There was only one decision that he needed to make and he needed to make it quickly. He needed to think of a place to take her for lunch where they wouldn't be seen.

CHAPTER 29

Horace and his outreach committee had found an old motel on the edge of downtown that was perfect for Noah's House. It was in pretty bad shape and had sat vacant for the last few years. At one time, it had been a beautiful auto motel for folks traveling to Florida. Then it fell on hard times and became a cheap flop house. After that, according to Chief Sparks, it was a place for the hookers to take their clients. The rooms could be rented by the hour. Then it reverted even further to a drug house until the city and the police department had shut it down all together. The little motel was perfectly situated in yet another way. Several gay and lesbian couples had been quietly buying up the old Victorian homes around the motel and restoring them to pristine value.

The motel itself needed a lot of work. There were ten large rooms with private baths all on ground level built in a square around the swimming pool. The pool itself had not had water in it for well over a decade. It was almost beyond repair. There was no central air conditioning and heating. At one time there had been a little restaurant at the front of the motel next to the offices. The early estimates for purchase and remodeling far exceeded what Steele and Horace had originally planned. Steele had taken the numbers back to the Diocese and hit a brick wall. Even the Chief and Stone had told him that it simply was not affordable. The Bishop had given him the same response. They suggested that he keep looking for other properties that were more in line with their original estimates.

Horace and his committee were convinced that this was the best piece of property. It would be better for the teens to locate it close to a quietly developing gay and lesbian neighborhood. With ten rooms, they could accommodate twenty teens. They could accommodate girls as well as boys. Skipper from the homeless shelter projected they would open with twelve boys in residence and six girls. They would still have one or two empty rooms to meet unanticipated needs. They could covert the office and lobby area into a recreation center and gathering space. The restaurant could become a dining room and kitchen. Horace had pleaded with Steele to try again with the Vestry and the Bishop. He did, but with the same results.

Steele was sitting in his office going over the projected income from the Chadsworth Alexander Endowment. He worked and reworked the numbers. He had committed funds to the Soup Kitchen, Duke's House for Homeless Men Living with Aids, to the Free Medical Clinic, and to Horace's compensation. Even if the investment were to increase by ten percent, he still would not have enough left to purchase the motel, remodel it, staff it and commit to the operations for the immediate future. "Dear God," he prayed. Please show me the way."

Horace Drummond was on the intercom. "Let's build Noah's House." His voice was melodic with his baritone chuckle.

"You sly fox," Steele shouted. "You've figured out a way for us to do it."

Horace broke into a full laughter. "And the same to you, Reverend Father. What makes you think so?"

"I can tell by the smug tone of your voice. You may talk like you've swallowed an altar rail, but I know you, my brother. You can't keep a secret from me."

"Well, you owe me."

"Oh?"

"Last night at dinner I was pouring it all out to Almeda. I told her about our vision for the motel. Then I showed her the numbers. She said she'd pay for it! Can you believe that? She said she'd pay for the purchase and the complete cost of the renovations. We only have to budget for the operations."

"Oh my God, Horace. You're married to a saint."

"I wouldn't go that far, but I think she's pretty fantastic right now."

"Horace, can she afford it?"

Horace roared with laughter. His laughter was so loud that Steele had to hold the telephone away from his ear. When he finally calmed down he chuckled, "Sometime when we've both had too much to drink I'll tell you just how much the woman really does have. Believe me Steele, this is petty cash for her. It's nothing."

Steele shook his head. "Brother, it may be petty cash to her, but it's going to be a home for twenty young people who have no home of their own."

The motel renovation did not take as long as they projected. The Bishop came to Falls City for the dedication. Steele had not notified the newspaper or the television stations. The safety of the teens came first. It was all very low-key. The Bishop walked through each room and blessed it with holy water. Almeda made arrangements for a catered reception. The invited guests consisted of the Vestry of First Church, the Diocesan Council, the staff at the homeless shelter and the new residents and staff of Noah's House. Howard Dexter and Elmer Idle were conspicuously absent. It didn't matter to Steele. That cold south Georgia night, ten boys and four girls that had been disowned by their own parents because they were gay slept in the comfort and safety of warm beds. As far as Steele Austin was concerned, they had done exactly what Jesus himself would have done. He reclined in his own bed that night in his new home in Magnolia Plantation. He gathered his wife in his arms and held her tight. His children slept soundly in their own rooms. He thanked God over and over again for his many blessings until his prayers were lost in a deep slumber.

CHAPTER 30

Meal times at the Mudd household had become strained. While the outward appearances were still present, the close family warmth was gone. Shady had noticed it. Shady's parents had been the household staff for Virginia Mudd's parents. They had lived in a small cottage behind the large house that Virginia and her family occupied. She and Virginia had played together as little girls. On the days she came to work for Henry and Virginia, she prepared breakfast just as she had always done. Something just was not right. There were no displays of affection between Henry and Virginia. There was little, if any, conversation at the table. Their two daughters appeared sullen and withdrawn. She had noticed that Henry had moved into a separate bedroom. Even Henry's blessing before breakfast was perfunctory and matter of fact.

"Virginia." It was as though Henry was looking at his wife without seeing her. "You have a conference with the girl's teachers today?"

Virginia nodded. "Yes, it's today."

"Good. I want to know why their grades are slipping. These two girls have always been excellent students. I just don't know what's happening over there at that school. If you can't get a satisfactory answer, I'll have a word with the Headmaster. It just seems to me that when the teacher fails to teach, the student fails to learn. We will get to the bottom of this."

Henry's two daughters looked at each other and sank down in their dining room chairs. "Sit up, girls," Virginia scolded. "Eat your breakfast." Virginia did not tell Henry that she'd already talked to the Headmaster. He had called to tell her that their oldest daughter had been in a fight with another girl in the locker room at school. Virginia just couldn't believe that one of her daughters had actually been in a physical struggle with another girl.

Shady drove the two girls to First Church School. Henry stayed at the dining room table reading the morning newspaper and drinking his coffee. When Virginia was sure that they were alone she asked, "Henry, what are we going to do?"

"About what?" He didn't even bother to look up from the newspaper.

"About us, Henry. What about you and me?"

This time he dropped the paper and looked at her. "I didn't realize that there was a decision to make. Or perhaps, you wanted to tell me that you'd gone out and gotten yourself knocked up by another Frenchman."

The words stung Virginia Mudd. She flinched as though he'd actually struck her with his hand. "Henry, I think the girls are letting their studies go because they know things are not right between us."

"And just when did you get your degree in psychology?" He smirked.

"Henry, say what you want, but the girls aren't buying our explanation for separate bedrooms."

"Oh?"

"No, they're not. Yesterday they asked me again. I explained that it was all due to my snoring problem. They gave each other a knowing look and then looked back at me with looks of disbelief. As they walked away they smarted back at me, 'Sure, Mom, whatever you say.' "

"Well, that's our story and we're sticking to it. They'll get used to it." He picked up his paper and started reading again.

"Henry, please put down the paper. We've got to talk this through. I'm trying. I'm really trying. I've told you a thousand times just how sorry I am. I made a mistake. I did something really stupid. I admit it. Can't you find it in your heart to forgive me?"

He put down the paper and stared coldly at her. She could feel the anger and hatred well up in him. "And then what? What do we do if I do forgive you? Just where do we go from there?"

"We could go to marriage counseling. Perhaps we could have an even better marriage than we had before."

"And marriage counseling is going to help me forget the sight of you sitting naked on top of that frog? Just how am I supposed to ever get those images out of my mind, Virginia? Every time I close my eyes I can see you lying to me and sneaking off to take off your clothes so you could be with him. How, Virginia? How am I supposed to ever forget that?"

"Then maybe we should get a divorce."

Henry smirked, "Oh, that's what you think you want, do you?" He folded the newspaper and threw it on the floor. "Well, let me tell you exactly what that's going to look like. I'll bring out the pictures, the videos, the taped conversations of your love talk and just how much you missed him and needed him. I'll bring it all out. They'll be played in court and everyone sitting in that courtroom will see and hear them. I'll make sure that a reporter is there from the newspaper and both television stations. Now, tell me again about that divorce you want."

Virginia dissolved into tears. She lay her head down on the table. She sobbed, "You wouldn't do that, Henry. You wouldn't do that to the girls."

Henry stood and put on his suit coat. He took one last sip of his coffee and stared down at her. "Just try me, Virginia. Just try me."

"Henry can't you see you've created a living hell for me? I can't keep on living like this."

Henry screamed at her. "I didn't create this hell, Virginia. You did. You and your Frenchman did. You are the one that ruined our lives. I have to live with your sin every day of my life and by damn, Virginia, until the day I take my dying breath, you're going to live with it too!"

Her face was red and swollen with tears. She pleaded with him, "Henry, there's just got to be a better way."

He opened his brief case that Shady had left for him on top of the dining room buffet. He took out a newspaper and handed it to her. "Here, you might just find the cover story of the Raleigh, North Carolina newspaper amusing." He then stormed out of the house.

Virginia wiped her eyes and struggled to focus on the print. She immediately saw Jacque's picture. Then she saw the picture of the bloody bed.

CHAPTER 31

Steele was being pelted with rumors about the house that he and Randi had purchased in Magnolia Plantation. They were coming from every direction. Even the Presbyterians and Baptists were fueling the gossip. "Did you hear that the Rector of First Church paid over a million dollars for his new home in Magnolia Plantation?"

"Oh, you haven't heard the half of it. I understand that they gave every stick of furniture they had in the Rectory to The Good Will. And the Vestry bought them all new furniture to go in their fancy new home."

"You don't say."

"I do say. I have a friend that works at the Drexel Heritage Furniture Store. She told me herself. The Rector and his wife went in there and picked out over a hundred thousand dollars worth of their finest furniture and charged it all to First Church."

"Well, I do think that's just a bit much."

"If I were a member of that congregation, I'd be absolutely furious. Can you imagine taking the tithes and offerings of the widows and using them to buy the preacher a million dollar house?"

"And a hundred thousand dollars worth of furniture as well."

"I understand that a lot of the people at the church have canceled their contributions. They're refusing to give one red cent to the church until this situation gets corrected."

"I know that to be true. I was talking to one of the staff members, that cute little Judith Idle."

"Isn't she just darling?"

"She is at that. She and her husband are the backbone of that church. They both work so hard over there. You know she's such a fine Christian."

"He is too. He's just a wonderful man. They're both so devoted to the Lord."

"I know you're right. I just know that you are."

"Anyway, I was talking to her the other day. You remember, I said she was on the staff of the church so she'd know all that's going on over there first-hand. She says that the women of the church just can't stand that Rector's wife. They all think she's just so full of herself."

"Well, she is a real pretty woman. And she always looks so nice."

"Um hmmm, but that's the problem. They're wondering just where she gets the money to dress the way she does. I mean, you start watching. She wears some real expensive clothes."

"You know, I have noticed that. My husband is an excellent provider, but I just don't think I could keep up with her wardrobe. No one can figure out how he keeps her dressed in designer clothes on a preacher's salary."

"Now you see my point. Judith Idle says that her husband is on the Vestry and he's going to get them to look into it all."

"How are they going to do that?"

"Well, I guess there's some conversation around the Rector's expense account."

"They give their preacher an expense account?"

"Well, we do too. It's for entertaining the various organizations in the church like the women's group and so on. Doesn't your church do that?"

"No, I don't think so, but then we Baptists tend to keep a closer eye on our preachers than you Presbyterians and Episcopalians do. We don't let them get by with much. Every cent that the church spends has to be first approved by the entire congregation."

"I see. That's right interesting. Anyway, as I was saying, they're going to investigate to make sure that he's not using his expense account to buy his wife some of those fancy clothes."

"Seems to me that I recall they've investigated him several times before."

"Some say they just haven't looked hard enough. Judith says that this time they're going to take a close look at everything."

"Well, I know that our congregation wouldn't stand for our preacher to buy such a big house in a gated community."

"I know. Now why would you want to live in a neighborhood with a guard at the gate unless you had something to hide?"

"I agree. I couldn't agree more."

"It does make you wonder, doesn't it?

"Do the Rector and his wife have any close friends over there?"

"My understanding is that Almeda Alexander...remember she was married to that real good looking Chadsworth..."

"Oh, I do—I do. That was one of the best looking men I've ever seen in my life. I could just sit and stare at him all day."

"Now, now...you're a married woman. You remember he killed himself in a hotel bathroom in Atlanta."

"Tragic...just tragic...did they ever find out why he killed himself?"

"Oh, I heard that he'd lost a fortune in business and just couldn't take it. But I don't suppose any one really will ever know."

"Almeda seems to be living quite comfortably."

"They think he left her a fistful of life insurance policies. Anyway, as I was saying, Almeda and her, you know—new husband."

"Oh, sure, she married that...'

"Um hmmm...well, they are best friends with the Rector and his wife. Beyond that, my sources tell me they don't have any friends."

"Has anyone in the church actually seen the house that they bought?"

"Well, like I said, it's a gated community and unless a resident authorizes you to come in, you can't get past the guard at the gate."

"That's such a shame. I believe if I was a member of that church I'd find a way to get in there and at least get a look at what my tithe was buying."

"I agree. I agree. I suppose it's going to happen. You realize that the entire town is talking about this. Everywhere I go people are talking about the big mansion that the Rector of First Church and his wife have bought."

"Oh, you can't go anywhere without hearing about it."

"True, so true...but you know the best part."

"What's that?"

"As long as folks are talking about the Episcopalians they're not talking about us Baptists and Presbyterians."

"That is good news, isn't it?"

CHAPTER 32

Father Austin, this is Stephen over at Noah's House."

"Yes, Stephen." Stephen Fox had been one of the case workers at the Homeless Shelter. Skipper recommended him to Steele and Horace to be the resident director of Noah's House when it opened. Stephen had his Master's Degree in Social Work from the University of Florida. He and his wife lived at Noah's House. When they had a day off or wanted a vacation, Skipper Hodges at the shelter loaned one of his other case workers to Noah's House.

"Father Austin, the television cameras are all over us. They're doing a story on Noah's House. There's a reporter from the newspaper here as well. He keeps asking me if we're providing a place for young boys to have homosexual sex. He's suggesting this is just a glorified bath house for gay sex. I don't know what to do."

Steele felt the panic in the pit of his stomach. He knew that unless he cooperated fully the press would spin the story so as to get the most mileage out of it. "Show them around. Open all the doors. We have nothing to hide. Tell them that I'll be over there in just a few minutes. I will be happy to give them a complete interview. Invite them into the recreation room and offer them some snacks and drinks. Above all, stay calm."

When Steele arrived at Noah's House the reporters and camera men ran at him. "Father Austin, are you encouraging teenagers to have gay sex in this motel?"

"Ladies and gentlemen, let's turn off the cameras for just a minute. Let's sit down and talk. Let me give you some background and then I'll answer all your questions on or off camera."

"Promise?"

"Promise."

They all agreed. Everyone took a seat in the recreation room. Skipper Hodges from the Homeless Shelter arrived just after Steele did. "You all know Skipper Hodges. He's the director of the Homeless Shelter. I'd like to start by having him share some information with you on the number of homeless teens on the streets of Falls City. I'd like for him also to tell you how the Homeless Shelter has tried to meet their needs. I'll pick it up from there."

After Skipper had finished, Steele then told them how Noah's House was a partnership between First Church, The Diocese of Savannah, and The Chadsworth Alexander Endowment. He told them that they had tried to keep it all low key and out of the press for the safety of the residents. He begged them to cooperate so that these homeless teens could have a safe place to live. He got all of them to agree not to include the location of Noah's House in their reports. They would treat it as they would any other safe house. Then the questions began.

"Father Austin, why did you choose a motel? You realize that this was once a flop house for prostitutes and their clients?"

"How can you be sure that the teens aren't engaging in homosexual sex? You do have two gay boys and two lesbian girls sharing a room."

"Why would the Episcopal Church want to provide housing for homosexuals? Don't you think it's a sin?"

"Are you trying to cure these young people of their homosexuality? Don't you think Jesus would try to heal them? Don't you agree the Bible is clear that homosexuality is a sin?"

Steele and Skipper tried to answer each of their questions. They tried to keep them focused on the fact that if it weren't for Noah's House all of these young people would be living on the streets. They had three things in common. They had been disowned by their parents. They were homeless. And they were gay. Noah's House was a ministry created primarily because they were homeless and had no place to go. Would the members of the press prefer that they be on the streets, sleeping in the parks and under bridges? He concluded by appealing to them to share in this ministry and to protect these young people's anonymity and safety.

Steele and Randi waited for the eleven o'clock news that night with fear and trepidation. Their first clue that the press was going to put their own spin on things was when they heard the announcer's voice say, "On the local news tonight, SNews investigates whether or not a local motel is a safe place for teenagers to live, or is it just a safe place for them to engage in gay sex?"

"Oh, God, please don't let them do this," Steele prayed.

The reporter was standing in front of Noah's House. While she did not disclose the location, most of the residents nearby would easily be able to identify it. The next camera shot was of one of the rooms. The camera focused on the twin beds in the room. "Each room is secured with a lock from the inside. Two gay males or gay females reside in each room. This ministry to these teenagers is being sponsored by First Episcopal Church. The Rector, Father Austin, assures SNews Investigative Reporters that he does not encourage homosexual sex or any kind of sex among teenagers. We here at your news service plan to stay on top of this story."

The telephone rang as soon as the reporter signed off. "They betrayed us, Steele." It was Horace and he was furious. "Their entire story was about providing a place for gay sex. They didn't even mention the fact that these kids have been disowned by their parents or that they're homeless. This is not good, brother. This is not good."

"I know. I just don't know what to do." Randi brought Steele a Scotch and water. He nodded and mouthed a thank you. "I guess we just sit back and hope it all blows over. I'll talk to you tomorrow."

He had no more than hung up when the phone rang again. "Steele, this is Rufus Petersen. What the hell is going on down there?"

"I wish I could tell you. I still don't know how they even found out about Noah's House. Although...I have a couple of good hunches."

"I'll bet we have the same two hunches. You need to fire one of them."

"I know, but it's not that easy when her husband is on my Vestry."

"Take it from your Bishop, Steele. That man is no friend of yours. Keep me informed."

"I'll do it. Please excuse me, Bishop I have another call waiting for me."

Steele disconnected from the Bishop and heard a familiar and comforting voice on the call that was waiting. "I'm sending one of my officers over there to spend the night."

"Thanks, Chief. I'll let Stephen, the Director over at Noah's House know."

"I'm not sending a uniform. He'll be in an unmarked car. He'll show them his badge."

"Thanks, I really appreciate it."

"I don't need to tell you that this is only the beginning."

"I just hope this runs its course, and fast."

"I wouldn't count on that."

Steele and Randi both had a restless night. Steele turned on the early morning news and his worst fears were realized. The television reporter was standing in front of a group of demonstrators carrying signs. They were chanting "Close it down. It's a House of Sin. Close it down. It's a House of Sin." They were carrying signs with Bible quotes on them and other slogans condemning homosexuality. The telephone rang. It was the Chief. "I've got my men over there. They'll keep the demonstrators on the other side of the street."

"Thanks, Chief. I really appreciate it."

"I fear that I have to tell you something else."

"Oh?"

"I just got a call from the Mayor. He wants me to shut you down."

"Do you have to do that? I mean...we have all the necessary permits. Everything is in order."

"No, as long as you meet the requirements of the law, I don't have any grounds, but he tells me that he's being swamped with phone calls and messages. All of them want you closed down. He says that the Christians for Moral Purity are going to file a lawsuit to get you closed down. You just need to make sure that those teens are the perfect example of moral purity until this goes away. I don't care if you have to put Salt Peter in all their potatoes. Make sure that nothing is going on over there that some nosy reporter can blow out of proportion."

"I'll take care of it."

"Chief, we don't have the funds to defend ourselves against a law suit. You and I both know the Vestry will never fund a defense. The Bishop sure won't pay for it. I just don't know what we're going to do."

"One day at a time, Parson. One day at a time."

After he hung up, Steele turned the volume up on the television. The reporter was interviewing one of the protestors. "Homosexuality is a sin. The Episcopal Church should be ashamed of itself for buying a motel for these young Sodomites. This is a disgrace. If your viewers want to contribute to the fund to have this den of iniquity shut down, then call Christians for Moral Purity."

The reporter indicated that the number to call would be shown on the viewer's television screen at the end of this broadcast.

Steele felt Randi's hand on his shoulder. She handed him a cup of coffee. "It's really bad, isn't it?"

He nodded. "They're so focused on the fact that these kids are gay they are completely ignoring the fact that they're homeless. They have been disowned by their own parents. If Noah's House is shut down, they'll be back on the streets. Their only source of income will be drugs and prostitution. They're literally sentencing these poor kids to a certain death. But they don't seem to care about that. They'll quote the Bible condemning them for being gay as these poor kids take their last breath."

"I know you're right. It's just all so sad. What are you going to do?"

"I don't know. I just don't know."

Steele pulled into the staff parking lot at First Church. As he got out of the car, he looked up and he was blinded by a flash. A newspaper reporter and photographer had been waiting for him. "Father Austin, how do you justify housing homosexuals in a church owned motel?"

Steele stood and looked directly at the reporter. "And just where would you have these homeless teenagers live? Would you want one of your children homeless and living on the streets?"

"One of them is." The reporter shot back.

Steele was confused. "One of them is what?"

The reporter smirked. "I threw my lesbian daughter out of the house."

Steele shook his head. "You did what? How old is she?"

"She was fifteen at the time. The Bible makes it clear that homosexuals are an abomination to God."

Steele looked at the man. He showed absolutely no regret. He started to walk away, but he couldn't resist. "Tell me, what does the Bible say about a Father's love?"

CHAPTER 33

"You know that I'm going to have to fire you."

"Why, Henry Mudd, what are you talking about?" Dee knew he was teasing her. They were huddled together in their favorite corner booth at Daisy's Café. The café was located on the far south end of the town. It featured country cooking. The house special was a large chicken fried steak served with grits, fried okra, collard greens, and fried apples for dessert. It could all be washed down with your favorite American beer. Daisy did not serve foreign beers. The large American Flag hanging above the bar accented her choice for all things American. On Friday and Saturday nights, there was live country music. The various local bands rotated performance nights. On Sunday mornings, Daisy's Café was turned into a Cowboy Church. Those who preferred their Christianity dished up with fervent preaching and live country music were in attendance. Daisy reopened her establishment as a restaurant after services. The Sunday buffet included Country Ham, fried chicken, fried catfish and all the trimmings reminiscent of Sunday dinner at your mothers'.

"I'm going to have to fire you." Henry smiled. "I can't risk having you file a law suit against my firm for sexual harassment or some other nonsense."

"Henry, I would never do anything like that. So far the only thing we've done is have a few lunches together."

He reached under the table and squeezed her hand. She rubbed her leg against his. "The important part of that sentence is the *so far* part."

"I know. I feel the same way." She lifted his pants cuff with one of her feet and gently rubbed his leg with it."

He smiled at her and looked around the restaurant. He had chosen it because he was almost certain that they wouldn't see anyone they knew. As he looked over the patrons, he was even more certain that none of his friends from First Church or the Magnolia Club would even think of dining here. He'd discovered that Dee was on his mind all the time. He thought about her constantly. He still remembered the first time that their hands touched. It gave him a feeling that he'd never known before. He tried to tell himself it was ridiculous, even adolescent. Their hands only touched, but he had intentionally relived that instant in his mind over and over again. He loved talking to her. He loved the way she smelled. He had asked her for a picture. He'd hidden it in his desk drawer so that he could look at it when he missed her. And he did miss her. When they couldn't be together he longed to be with her. When they were apart he was almost paralyzed with loneliness. He hated weekends. "You have to stop."

"Oh, I'm sorry. I thought maybe you liked that."

Henry smiled at her. "Oh, I do. I like it every time you touch me. It's just that if you keep doing that I'm not going to be able to walk out of this restaurant."

She giggled. "So I do have some effect on you."

"You know you do. I love everything about you. That's why I'm firing you."

Her smile was replaced with a questioning look. "Are you serious? Are you really going to fire me?"

He nodded. "Dee, I'm not going to be able to keep this up. I just don't know how long I'm going to be satisfied with conversation and hand holding. I think I want more."

She nodded and rubbed his leg with her hand. "Me too, I'm crazy about you."

"It's all so complicated right now. I'm married and I have my two daughters to think about."

"But your wife cheated on you. You're married in name only."

"I know. We don't even sleep in the same bed. I'm repulsed by the very sight of her. The only thing I know for sure is that I love being with you. I just want some time to see where this is going."

"So what am I supposed to do if you fire me?"

He gave her a reassuring smile. "You're going to start working for the hospital as a receptionist. The hospital is one of my clients. I've already arranged for you to have the position."

"And, why do I think there's more to your plan?"

"Do you want to be a receptionist the rest of your life?"

"Of course not, I told you I wanted to be a paralegal."

"And so you shall. I've talked to the Dean of the College. He's going to give you a full scholarship. You'll begin night classes next week."

"It seems to me that you have my days and nights pretty heavily scheduled."

He smiled and put his arm around her shoulder. "Then I won't have to worry about some young gentleman sweeping you off your feet before I have a chance to do that myself."

"You already have."

Henry smiled. He was pleased to hear that she felt as he did. "Dee, I've got to have some time. I need to figure out just what I'm going to do about my marriage. I've got to really be careful. I won't hurt my girls."

She removed his arm from her shoulder. "I'll tell you what, Henry Mudd. You don't have to fire me. I quit!"

"Oh?"

"Don't get exercised. It sounds like I'm going to be pretty busy day and night the next couple of years. You take all the time you need to figure things out."

"Thanks, thanks for understanding."

"I appreciate the new job and the scholarship. You, Henry Mudd, are a class act."

They stood to leave the restaurant. He helped her slip into her jacket. She turned to face him. She put both of her hands on his chest and looked up into his eyes. "You know, I'm still going to need to eat lunch at that new job."

"And so we shall," he smiled.

"And what am I to do on the weekends? I get so lonely on the weekends."

"I do too. Let's figure out a way to do something about that as well." Then Henry Mudd wrapped his arms around her and pulled her tightly up against his body. He mustered up all of his self control. His intention was to just to kiss her lightly on the cheek. He failed.

CHAPTER 34

This parish is in turmoil, Father Austin." Just look at these letters. Elmer Idle was waving around a handful of letters and envelopes. "It's like we've gone from Palm Sunday to Good Friday in just a matter of weeks." Elmer's face grew so red Steele was afraid that his entire head was going to explode. "Father Austin, it wasn't that long ago that this congregation was celebrating the fact that you weren't going to leave us. We celebrated the birth of your daughter. And now look at these, read them! This congregation is after your hide."

Stone Clemons looked around the table. "I didn't get any letters from the congregation. Did any of you other boys receive any letters?" All present shook their heads. Stone shrugged.

"Well, I got some letters." Ned Boone's voice boomed off the conference room walls. He was once again sitting in the visitors section up against the wall. "I also have a petition with over one hundred names on it."

"What sort of petition?" Howard Dexter, the Senior Warden asked.

"It's a petition demanding that this congregation be given an accounting of the Rector's Expense Account. We want a full and open disclosure as to just where he's spent every penny of it since the day he arrived."

"Ned, I can't speak for everyone here, but I'm completely opposed to spending any more money on auditors. We have looked at everything multiple times already. With the exception of some disagreements over judgment and financial priorities, the Rector continues to come out beyond reproach."

"Well, what if you were to find out that he charged his expense account for a pearl and diamond bracelet for his wife?"

Steele glared at Ned. "Would you please tell me what you're talking about?"

"So you deny buying a pearl and diamond bracelet at Brown's Jewelry Store. Mind you, that's the most expensive jewelry store in town."

"No, I don't deny it. I bought it for Randi for our wedding anniversary. She doesn't even know about it yet. How did you find out I bought it?"

Ned smirked at Steele, "You just never mind that. The question is just how did you pay for it?"

"I wrote a check, but I really don't think that's your concern." Steele was trying to keep his irritation under control.

"On what account?"

"On my personal checking account, thank you."

"And you have the canceled check?"

"Well, not yet. I just wrote it yesterday."

"I insist that you call your bank and get me a copy of that check."

Steele could hold his anger no longer. "No sir, I will not. You have tried to get access to my personal financial records before. I'm telling you now what I told you then, they are none of your business."

"Calm down, let's just all calm down." Howard Dexter was motioning with his hands. "Ned, I'll have the treasurer pay special attention to the Rector's Expense Account this month. We'll look for any charges to Brown's Jewelry. Will that satisfy you?"

"Well, a lot of the people in this Church want to know just how the Rector affords to live so high on the hog." Elmer Idle was rapidly firing his words at Steele.

Steele just shrugged. He chose not to comment.

"You can sit over there looking all smug if you want, but the people in this church pay your salary. We do it with our hard-earned contributions. The women of this church want to know just how you can afford to keep your wife in designer dresses and buy her pearl and diamond bracelets."

Again, Steele chose not to dignify his comments with a response.

"You may not realize it, Father Austin, but everyone at this table is aware that your house is the talk of this town. We are all absolutely embarrassed for you and for this church. You drove a hard bargain on your housing allowance. We should have stood our ground against you."

Steele could feel the anger welling up inside him, but sat in silence.

"Are we ready to move on with Vestry business?" Chief Sparks asked.

"This is Vestry business!" Ned Boone exploded.

"No, it's really not." Stone Clemons ruled. "The Rector's personal finances are not the concern of this body."

"Well, I do agree that a diamond and pearl bracelet is a bit of an extravagance." Howard Dexter smiled. "The only diamond I've ever given my wife was on her engagement ring and that was almost forty years ago. I would think you need to be a bit more cautious about your choice of gifts for your wife."

Stone grinned, "Howard, are you trying to tell us that with all the money you have, you've only bought your wife one diamond in forty years of marriage?"

Howard nodded. He was quite pleased with himself. "That's the only piece of jewelry I've ever bought her."

Stone returned his smile. "I just don't think I would have told that in a public gathering." Everyone at the table roared with laughter. Everyone, that is, except Elmer and Ned.

Howard tried to direct the Vestry back to the business at hand. "Father Austin, we do have to address the concerns being expressed in the congregation about the motel you opened for the homosexuals."

"I know, but let's call it Noah's House. And let's stay focused on the fact that it's a safe house for homeless teenagers."

"Well, that may be, but the press is not doing you any favors. I received a telephone call from the Bishop this afternoon. He advises me that unless we can avert a law suit, he will not be able to honor his commitment. Now that's one third of the cost of that project."

Steele nodded, "I know. He called me as well."

Elmer seized on the moment. "I make a motion that this Vestry cancel our support." There was no immediate second at the table.

"Misturh Austin, I fear that Elmer is correct. I'm going to have to second his motion unless you give me some convincing arguments to the contrary."

"I understand how everyone at this table must feel. It's all really frustrating. The press has not done us any favors. They've rallied people who are so fixated on homosexuality that they're blind to their own sins."

"What sins?" Ned Boone's voice once again filled the conference room.

Steele tried to keep his own voice calm. "Ned, these young people are just children. Some of them are only fourteen or fifteen years old. They are homeless. They've been disowned by their families. They have no suitable way to support themselves. Now for the followers of Jesus to turn our backs on them is a sin."

"That's just a lot of liberal bleeding heart dribble." Ned shot back.

Henry Mudd leaned across the table to look directly at Ned. "I don't presume to know the Bible as well as the Rector, but I do recall that on the final Day of Judgment, one of the questions that Jesus will ask us is whether or not we gave him a shelter when he had none."

"Now you're not trying to tell us that Jesus was a homosexual, are you?" Ned smirked.

Henry threw his arms in the air and looked over at Stone.

Stone nodded, "I know that the suit has been filed. I will pledge to put some of my attorneys on it initially. We'll do it pro-bono."

"I'll have a couple of my boys work with yours, Stone. We'll do it under the same terms," Henry added.

"Thanks, guys," Steele smiled. "That will buy us some time and allow us to continue to house these kids until we can come up with a better plan."

"The best plan would be to send these kids back to their parents." Elmer slumped down in his chair. Clearly, his motion was going to die for the lack of a second.

Howard Dexter looked over at Steele. "Misturh Austin, this Vestry is going to stay with you for now on this project. You need to know that support for it is dying. I suggest that you and Dr. Drummond figure out a way to get it out of the news and out of the courts. If you fail to do so, we'll all be forced to reconsider our support."

Steele nodded. "I understand. I just want to thank you on behalf of all those kids. Thanks for giving us some time to solve the problem."

As Steele drove home, he felt so helpless. In his heart he knew that, short of a miracle, there would be no way for him to save Noah's House. Those poor kids would be back on the streets with only the homeless shelter giving them periodic relief. By the time he pulled into his driveway he was exhausted, but that night he wasn't able to sleep.

CHAPTER 35

He put down his morning newspaper so that he could watch the young man on the treadmill. They'd been together for well over three years now. He loved watching him. The muscles in his legs and back were so smooth. His body was the kind photographers craved to photograph and sculptors strived to duplicate in clay. He liked watching him exercise. "How much longer are you going to be running on that thing?

"Another thirty minutes. You know, you could use some exercise yourself. I've been noticing a spare tire is beginning to inflate around your mid section."

"I could run on that thing all day and it wouldn't help. I know exactly what I have to do. I've already made an appointment with the best plastic surgeon in the city."

"Isn't there a limit to the number of liposuctions one man can have?"

"Do you want me to look good or not?"

The young man stopped the treadmill and looked back at him. He shot him a wide white-toothed smile. "You always look good to me." Then he turned on the treadmill and started running again.

The penthouse apartment in San Francisco that he had bought soon after his arrival in the city was well situated on Nob Hill. He had a clear circular view of the surrounding area. In the distance he could see the Golden Gate and Sausalito. Grace Cathedral was visible as was the Fairmount Hotel. Below he could see a large procession making its way through one of the streets. He had come to recognize such an occurrence as a Chinese funeral procession. On the balcony just below him, he saw two young women embrace, kiss each other and then stretch out on two leisure chairs to read their magazines. He so envied the young people today. They had been able to come out and accept their sexuality so early in their lives. Here in this city they were free to be who they were. He winced at the thought of all the years that he had spent living a double life. He'd really believed that if he got married he would be able to change. He'd dismissed his attraction for members of his own sex as adolescent confusion. He could not silence the fantasies he kept having about other men. Then he remembered that just two weeks into his marriage, he'd sought out a male escort.

Living two lives had not been easy for him. With his wife and children, he'd been able to present his best face to society. Still, he'd lived in constant fear that his secret would be discovered. There were so many close calls. He'd been arrested a couple of times. He got lucky both times and was able to keep the arrests secret. .He was happiest when he could be himself. His long-term lover made him happy. Just being with him made him happy. When he was with him and all their friends in Atlanta, there was no pretense. There was no need to keep up a front. He could be himself. The young people today, in a city like this, will never have to live a double life. He wished that he could be young again. He wished that he'd been free to be himself from the beginning. He so wished that he could have it to do over. A thousand times he'd told himself there was no use crying over what might have been. He was determined to be thankful for the life he was now able to live. He was determined to celebrate every day of it.

He had learned so much about how other people like him had lived with their secrets. Just last night they'd attended an anniversary party for two women in the condo directly below theirs. The two women were celebrating their fiftieth year together. For most of their lives they had to pretend to be sisters in their small town in Nebraska. Most everyone had accepted their story. They were just two old maid school teachers living together. The fact that they were *sisters* made it all the more acceptable. When they retired they moved to San Francisco and openly claimed the life they'd lived in secret. He'd met so many men and women that had been faithfully committed to each other for decades.

He glanced again at his partner who was now jogging at top speed on the treadmill. The muscles in his arms and back were so well defined. His calves looked as though they were going to explode. When he first met him he was one of the Circuit Boys. He'd actually met him at the White Party in Palm Springs. He'd gone out of curiosity as much as anything else. It was his first experience with a Circuit Party. He'd heard about the Circuit Boys that would go from weekend event to weekend event around the country. The parties on the Circuit were the largest gatherings of gay men in America. The biggest ones were in San Francisco, New York, and Boston. Palm Springs was the largest of them all. Most referred to it as the diamond in the belt.

He hadn't expected to make a serious connection with anyone. Most of the Circuit Boys were there just for the good time and nothing more. He spotted him at the Saturday night dance. It was an incredible experience. Over five thousand shirtless men crowded the convention center to dance the night away. Their eyes met. They returned each other's smiles. He asked him to dance. That night this new blonde Adonis in his life ceased to be a Circuit Boy. A few months later in a ceremony in Hawaii, he became his life partner.

Since that day, they'd settled into a routine that was reminiscent of his former life as a married man. Their daily activities consisted of cooking and cleaning. They'd spent weeks decorating their new home. They planned vacations, played golf and tennis. They were active in the Cathedral congregation. They volunteered for charitable organizations. Small dinner parties they could host brought them special pleasure. Arguments surrounded music and art preferences, politics and religion. Occasionally each of them would get jealous if they suspected the other was flirting with an attractive person. And just like every other couple in the world, once the initial passion had worn off, their bedroom was used primarily for sleeping.

He picked up the newspaper and began reading again. Then a small article on the third page caught his eye. It was from Falls City, Georgia. The story was captioned, "SAFE HOUSE FOR HOMELESS TEENS THREATENED." It was a very brief article only three paragraphs long. It reported that activists on both sides from around the nation were watching the events unfold in the small south Georgia community. Christians for Moral Purity were attempting to close down a homeless shelter for gay and lesbian teenagers that had been started by the Episcopal Church. The Rector of the local parish, The Reverend Steele Austin, had reported that they simply did not have the funds to fight the litigation.

He closed the newspaper and stared out the window for a few minutes. He looked back at his partner, who was still running on the treadmill. "Can you turn that off for a minute? I need to make a phone call."

CHAPTER 36

Bud, how's school going?" Steele and Randi had been invited by Almeda to join Horace, Bud and her for Sunday brunch. Almeda had her *help* set up a table by the pool behind their house. A starched white table cloth covered the table. She had placed a beautiful arrangement of flowers from Albert Rawlins in the center of the table. The china that she used only for her outside events was from Royal Doulton. The adults began with a pre-dinner drink. It was one of Almeda's signature drinks that she only presented to her very special dinner guests. It was served in a globe shaped wine glass. There was a fresh peach half in the bottom of the glass with a maraschino cherry nestled in its heart. The peach had been marinating for most of the morning in an ample amount of Southern Comfort. When the time to serve the drink arrived, she instructed the bartender to pour cold champagne in the glass. It made a colorful and tasty drink. She always served it with a cocktail napkin and a spoon. Many of her guests confessed that the best part of the drink was when they were able to finally eat the peach and the cherry. She would politely caution them that they probably did not want to have more than one. The peach did carry an extra punch.

"I like my school just fine, Father Austin."

Almeda cooed. "Bud has the lead in the school play. It's a musical. You should hear him sing. He has a beautiful voice."

"Have you thought about singing in the choir?" Randi smiled.

"I would, but I really like sitting with Almeda in church. You should sit with us. I see you over there all by yourself."

"Well, I have Travis with me and sometimes he gets a little restless."

"Nonsense, Randi." Almeda indicated for her cook to begin serving the plates. "We'd love to have you and Travis join us."

"And you don't think that the parish gossips would start talking about the priest's wives sitting together?" The cook sat Randi's plate down in front of her. It had a shrimp wrap on it and some green salad with a raspberry vinaigrette dressing. "This looks wonderful, Almeda."

Almeda smiled, "I just wanted to have something light today. I thought surely this would be suitable. I especially wanted you to save room for dessert. I made it myself. It's an old family recipe."

"Sounds intriguing," Randi hummed.

Horace chuckled. "Oh, all the ingredients are listed in the name."

"Oh?" Steele was now curious.

"Chocolate Coca Cola Cake." Horace continued to chuckle. "Only Almeda pronounces it Chocolate Co-cola Cake."

"Are you making fun of me?" Almeda shot a teasing look at Horace.

"Of course not, my darling. You know that I love you."

"And I love you. Now say the blessing or there'll be no Chocolate Co-cola Cake for you."

After the blessing Almeda frowned, "As for the gossips, I've learned to ignore them and you need to learn to do so as well."

Randi grimaced. "That really is easier said than done."

Almeda patted Randi's hand. "Listen to me. You're a beautiful woman with a handsome husband and two adorable children. You have good taste in clothing. Now you live in a wonderful new house in an exclusive part of town. Randi, some of these women are going to be jealous of you and there's nothing that you can do about it."

Steele shook his head. "So what you're telling us is that if Randi would dress in flour sacks, try to look homely, and we lived in a shack, then we wouldn't be a target?"

"Brother, you know better than that." Horace counseled. "You're the Rector of the church. You live in a glass house. It doesn't make any difference whether it's a Rectory or your own home. It could be a shack or a mansion and nothing would change. The walls of a clergy houses are made of glass. You two just need to be yourselves and ignore the gossips. You can't do anything about them anyway."

"But Horace," Randi was on the verge of tears. "If we could just explain to them why we wanted our own home maybe that would help. We chose the house that we did for our children."

This time it was Horace that put his hand on Randi's. "My grandmother was a very wise woman. She used to tell me that I never needed to justify myself to anyone. She told me not to ever fall into the trap of trying to explain myself or my decisions. Her wisdom was that your true friends do not require an explanation and your enemies won't believe anything you have to say anyway."

Steele gave a low whistle. "That's so true, isn't it?"

Almeda signaled to have the plates removed from the table. "Are you all ready for dessert?" After the dessert was served and the coffee poured, Almeda indicated for every one to eat. "Steele, do you have any new thoughts on how to save Noah's House?"

"Stone Clemons and Henry Mudd have both volunteered their firms to defend us for the short term. I think the only thing we've done is buy some time. Those people are relentless and clearly the press is not going to help us. I have to confess I'm not very hopeful. I wish we could find all the kids a home like you folks are providing for Bud."

Bud had not spoken all through dinner. He'd preferred to listen to the adult conversation. Steele turned to look at Bud. He was clearly Almeda's handiwork now. His hair was absent the streak of blonde and was cut short. He now had a small gold earring in one of his ears. He had a beautiful gold bracelet and a new watch on his wrists. Steele guessed they were gifts from Almeda. He was wearing kaki pants, a white dress shirt with a maroon tie, and a blue blazer. Steele couldn't see his feet but he knew that if he could Bud would be wearing Bass Weejuns. Steele's hunch was that he was not wearing socks with his Weejuns. It was the trademark of southern teens of class and breeding. "I owe my life to Almeda and Horace."

"What's next for you, Bud?"

"Mister Clemons tells me that he will help me get my emancipation. I think that's the only way that I can begin my life free of my parents' condemnation. Of course, I hope that one day they'll have a change of heart, but I don't have a lot of hope. They're getting their beliefs about gays reinforced every Sunday morning."

"Have you heard from them?"

Bud shook his head. "No, but that really is okay. I'm the happiest I've ever been in my life. I love Almeda and Horace. This is my home now."

"If I could ask one question, Almeda." Randi was hesitant. "How have your sons received Bud?"

Almeda shot Horace a look. "Well, as you might expect, they weren't too happy about Bud moving in here. Of course, their primary concern was whether or not Bud would be sharing in their trust funds. I was so disappointed in them. But then that's not new. They continue to find ways to disappoint me."

"Now, Almeda, they're not as bad as you make them out to be." Horace interjected.

"I don't know. They're just so consumed with money. Anyway, once I explained to them that their trusts were secure, they calmed down. They're not excited about Bud living here, but then I don't think they're going to cause any problems."

"They're nice enough to me." Bud smiled. "I mean, they treat me okay."

"And who wouldn't? You're one of the sweetest boys I've ever met in my life. You make me so happy. Horace and I are so proud of you. We love you just like you were one of our very own children." Almeda leaned over and kissed Bud on the cheek. "You are our son and this will always be your home." She took one of Bud's hands. Horace took the other. They squeezed them and smiled at him. It was a tender moment. Steele looked around the table and realized that tears were welling up in the eyes of all present, including his own.

CHAPTER 37

"Father Austin, this is John White calling from Atlanta."

"Yes," Steele was trying to recall why the name sounded familiar.

"Father Austin, I'm the senior partner at White, Hall, Lindsay, and Mellon."

When Steele heard the firm's name he remembered that they were the ones that had set up The Chadsworth Alexander Endowment. "Yes, Mister White. Has something happened to the Alexander Endowment?"

"Quite to the contrary, Father; I have several pieces of real good news for you."

Steele sat back in his chair. Intuitively he felt himself relax. "I could use some good news."

"Yes, I've been reading about your travails down there in Falls City. The Atlanta papers just carried a couple of paragraphs on the suit filed against your safe house. I had some of the Falls City newspapers mailed to me. It doesn't sound like the press has been on your side at all."

"I'm afraid not." Steele replied.

"These stories used every hot button adjective and noun they could to describe your project and not a single one that would gain you any support."

"I agree. We gave them all the correct information and were completely open with them, but they put their own spin on it all."

"Well, I'm happy to report to you that you don't have to worry about that suit any longer."

Steele leaped to his feet. "What?" He realized that he had just screamed into the telephone. "I'm sorry. Please forgive me for yelling, but what do you mean?"

John White chuckled, "That's perfectly understandable, Father Austin. I'm just happy to report to you that your case was of particular interest to us. I realize that you did not ask us to do so, nor did you have any knowledge of our actions, but we chose to intervene."

Steele was puzzled. "I'm sorry, but is that legal? I mean we already have legal representation."

"Let me reassure you and your attorneys. We didn't take any kind of legal action. It seems that one of our partners was personally acquainted with the President of Christians for Moral Purity. He just wanted to see if maybe he could work out something with them."

"That was really nice of you guys. I really appreciate it." Steele was beginning to feel more and more relieved.

"Well, the best part is that we were able to reach an agreement with them, but it does require you to do a couple of things."

"Like what?"

"Well, first you have to give the residents of Noah's House transportation to the church of their choice on Sundays. The rub is that the Moral Purity people don't want the Episcopal Church to be the only church that the teens can attend."

Steele smiled, "Mister White, we're already doing that. Only about half of the teens are choosing to go to a church of any kind. Most of them are coming here to First Church, but we have a couple going to another church. That's not a problem for us. We're just happy to have them go to any church. But I will be shocked if any of them choose to go to a church that has a chapter of the Moral Purity."

John White smiled. "If any of them should choose to go to one of those churches, will you please call me? I will need to get my affairs in order. I think that will be a true sign that the end of the world is near."

Both men laughed, "Amen, Mister White. Amen."

"There is one more condition that must be met. If you meet this condition they will sign a binding agreement never to interfere in any way with the operations of Noah's House again."

"Oh, name it. This is an answer to prayer. All of these kids need Noah's House. There needs to be a Noah's House in every city in this nation."

"I couldn't agree more. The second part of the agreement we reached with them will require some work and some money. They want Noah's House remodeled so that every teen has a private bedroom and private bathroom. They don't want them sharing a room."

Steele grunted. "Oh, I don't know. We just don't have the money to do anything like that. That would really be expensive. I honestly don't think I could raise the money to get it done in the current environment. I'm not sure I could raise the money to do that even if I'd never heard of the Moral Purity Group."

"Would you agree to the plan if we could get it funded?"

Steele didn't even have to think about his response. "In a heartbeat, but where would the money come from?"

"We already have it. Father Austin, our firm will pay for the remodeling of Noah's House. Our only condition on the gift is that it be anonymous. We do not want any recognition. We simply want to give it. We will pay all the expenses for the project, regardless of cost. There will be no pre-set limit on our gift."

Steele was dancing around his office. "Thank you, thank you. Oh, God bless you. You're an answer to prayer. I can't thank you enough. You're going to make a lot of homeless teenagers very happy."

"So you agree to these two terms?"

"Do you want me to sign something?"

"Yes, the Moral Purity Group wants you to sign an agreement. I'll fax it down to you. You just sign it and fax it back."

"What about them? Are they going to sign anything?"

"I'll take care of that. I'll send you a copy of everything through overnight mail. They're willing to sign a binding agreement into perpetuity that their organization will never interfere with the operations of Noah's House as long as these terms are met. Further, they will defend it against attacks from any other organization so long as these two conditions are met. They will even release a statement to the press stating such. I'll fax you a copy of the press release. Our people drew it up and they agreed to it. For the first time, the press will have to print language that deals with homeless kids and not some tirade about homosexuality."

"Gosh, Mister White, I just can't thank you enough. I'd thought we would need a miracle to save this ministry to these kids and I believe God has just given us one. Thank you so very much."

"No thanks are needed, Father. It pleases me to be able to do this. I'll fax you the agreements and the press release. Have your attorneys down there look at them and then fax them back to me. I have two representatives of Moral Purity with me in the office right now. They've agreed to sign them today."

John White turned to look at the two men sitting at the end of his conference room table. They were all that he had expected they would be. Haircuts from a chop shop, plaid suits with mismatched shirts and bow ties. They were a step above crooked used car salesmen and a notch below slick television evangelists. "The two of you heard everything."

They nodded. They couldn't keep the greedy looks off their faces. "What about our money?" The saliva literally drooled from the corners of his mouth as he asked the question.

John White reached for a brown legal folder. "First, you have to sign this."

"I thought we agreed you'd pay us in cash."

"Oh, you'll receive cash, but before you get it you will need to sign these receipts." He handed each of them a multi-page document."

"What's this? This is no receipt. What are all these words?"

John was disgusted with these two Pharisees. Their holier than thou attitude angered him. He considered them to be bottom feeders of the worst kind. "By this document you both acknowledge that you have negotiated this agreement with Noah's House in Falls City. It also recognizes that you have each been paid a substantial fee in cash for your services. You also accept our terms that should you or any member of your organization ever interfere with the operations of Noah's House again, this agreement, including your names and services, will be made public. By signing this you refute your right ever to litigate against this firm or anyone associated with Noah's House. Beyond that, should you or your organization fail to honor every comma and period in this agreement, you will have to repay your management fees to us, plus an interest of twelve percent per year compounded annually. Do you understand?"

The two men looked at each other and literally rubbed their hands together like praying mantises ready to pounce on their victim. "Where do we sign?"

He slid the documents before each of them and gave them each a pen. Sign at the X and put your initials on each page. The two didn't even bother to read the documents. While they were still signing the documents, they both asked at the same time, "When do we get our cash?"

John White took the documents from them and examined each page to make sure they were signed correctly. He then reached into the legal folder and brought out two stacks of cash. He handed one to each man.

They greedily took them from him and started thumbing through them. "Now the government is not going to know about this money, right?"

"No one is going to know anything about it as long as you honor this agreement.

The two men stood and eagerly shook John White's hand. Both of their palms were so sweaty he had to wipe his hand with a handkerchief when they left. He watched them go down the hall. They were slapping each other on the back. One of them let out a rebel yell. His secretary came into the conference room. "Who were those guys?"

John just shook his head. "Believe me, you don't want to know. I've got to go wash my hands. Will you call the maintenance staff and have them clean this conference room?"

"Mister White, it looks fine to me."

"No, it's really not. It's filled with the smells of moral superiority. I want it cleaned."

John would wash his hands several times over the next few days. He only found peace with himself when he confessed his arrangement with these two purists to his own parish priest. His priest counseled him to read again Jesus' constant encounters with the Pharisees, including his final encounter on Good Friday. Then his priest comforted him with these words, "Evil is never more dangerous than when it sees itself as good."

CHAPTER 38

The doorbell rang. Randi opened the front door only to come face to face with a very large flower arrangement. Standing behind the arrangement was a young man from Albert Rawlins Florist. "I have this delivery for The Reverend and Mrs. Steele Austin." Randi took the flowers, thanked the young man, and carried them into the dining room. She put the flowers in the middle of the dining room table. "Who are they from?" Steele asked.

Randi opened the envelope and read the note. Her eyes grew large and then she handed the note to Steele. "I don't believe it."

"Steele, what's going on?"

"I don't know. Maybe he really is trying to change."

"But Steele, they're quite beautiful. This is a very expensive flower arrangement."

Steele smiled. "Let's give Bishop Petersen the benefit of the doubt. Who knows, maybe God finally has been able to soften his heart of concrete. This really is a nice note. I'll call him and thank him for the flowers."

"No, Steele. If you think it would be acceptable, I'd like to call him."

Steele smiled at his wife. "You know what? I think that would be even better." He kissed his wife and went back to hanging pictures and curtains.

Randi was unpacking boxes in Travis' room. Her parents had given them a cash gift to hire a decorator to advise them on their various decorating alternatives. Rob and Melanie had paid the decorator to completely take care of Amanda and Travis' rooms. The walls in Amanda's room were done with the predictable pink, but the ceiling had three-dimensional clouds and stars hanging from it. Travis could not be happier with his room. The decorator had the walls covered with Disney characters. The headboard on Travis' bed was actually a very large Mickey Mouse. His arms were stretched out to make the sideboard. Travis said the Mickey was holding him when he went to sleep at night.

The decorator had really come up with some unique ideas for the living room and the dining room. Melanie was just a bit hesitant to use the dark greens and reds that he wanted to use on the walls. She finally relented when he countered, "Darling, you're living in *the South*. This is a southern home. You simply must take advantage of the good taste that these colors communicate."

Travis particularly liked eating outside on the deck behind the house. It overlooked the community lake. There were ducks on the lake. Travis liked to have Steele take him down to the lake to feed the ducks. If Travis had his way, they would have a picnic every day. In fact, he would take all three meals on the deck.

Amanda had developed a very predictable eating and sleeping routine. Randi's mother had taught her a little trick soon after Travis was born. She told her that as soon as Travis was able, she should give him a little rice cereal right before he went to sleep at night. His full tummy would help him sleep through the night. It was a welcome piece of advice. When Travis was ready, they started giving him the cereal. Sure enough, he started sleeping through the night. Amanda was now able to have a little rice cereal before she went to sleep. Now she too was sleeping through the night. It certainly made for an even happier household.

Steele was hanging the drapes in the dining room when he noticed a car driving very slowly past his house. He thought he recognized the driver. It was Elmer Idle. Judith was sitting in the backseat. She actually had a pair of binoculars up to her eyes. She was trying to look inside their house. The car came to a complete stop in the middle of the street. The passenger door opened and a man got out and lifted a camera to his face. He took several pictures of their house. It was Ned Boone. When he got back in the car they drove off. Steele waited. In just a few minutes the car passed their house again. Once again it was moving very slowly. This time Ned Boone was sitting in the back seat. He had the binoculars up to his eyes. The car stopped so that Ned could try to see in each of the windows.

CHAPTER 39

"Can you believe that house?"

Ned Boone, Judith and Elmer Idle had decided to finish off their little adventure by having lunch at Smitty's Grill. Smitty's Grill specializes in a sit-down service for fast food. The menu includes the usual hot dogs, hamburgers, B.L.T.s and grilled cheese served with a heaping order of French fries. Grilled pimento-cheese sandwiches are the hands down best sellers. Smitty's is a gathering place for all the teenagers, but in a twist of irony, it's also a favorite of the Country Club set.

"It's absolutely sinful!" Elmer shook his head. "That preacher ought to be ashamed of himself. Can you imagine using our contributions and our sacrificial offerings to purchase such a lavish house? I'd be embarrassed for him, but I don't think the man knows what it is to be embarrassed. I'm not sure he even has a conscience."

The disgust on Ned Boone's face was unmistakable. "Well, he may think he's pulling the wool over the eyes of the people in this parish. I'm going to make sure every member of our church gets a copy of these pictures. I'm going to pay for the mailing myself. Most folks won't go to all the trouble of trying to get past the guard at the gate to Magnolia Plantation to see that house. Well, we'll just bring the house to them."

"How will they know the house belongs to Austin?" Elmer asked.

"I'm going to enclose a note. 'Do you approve of the way your tithes and offerings are being spent?' I'm going to send it to every member listed in the parish directory."

Judith's eyes grew wide. "I don't think it's going to do any good. I know every woman that I talk to in the church is absolutely furious about that house. I can't stand his wife. She really thinks she's something. Now she has that big new house. Did you know they're having it professionally decorated?"

Ned sat back in his chair. "No. Where are they getting the money for that? Interior decorators are expensive."

"That's the question!" Elmer shot his words at Ned. "Where do they get the money for all that they do? Judith and some of her friends tell me that the total cost for Randi's clothes are more than we pay him."

"Well, we're going to find all that out." Ned tapped his finger on the table for emphasis.

Elmer shook his head. "Ned, I don't know. We've tried everything and he keeps coming out squeaky clean. I just don't know how we're ever going to be able to figure out how he finances his extravagant lifestyle."

"Well, you mark my word. I'm going to find out." Ned pushed his empty plate away from him.

"I have to agree with Elmer." Judith was twisting the napkin in her lap into a knot. "He appears to have Henry Mudd on his side and now it looks like even the Bishop has joined forces with him."

Elmer's face turned bright red. "Ned, did you hear about all the remodeling that's being done over at that homosexual motel?"

Ned nodded, "I heard. The entire place is being completely remodeled. I called Henry Mudd and asked him if he knew where Austin got the money for all that work. I mean, he just bought it and remodeled it once. Now, less than a month later, it's being completely remodeled again. Can you believe it? The man seems to have tapped into an endless supply of money."

"What did Henry tell you?" Elmer asked.

"What his cronies always tell us. It's all anonymous. I'm not satisfied with that answer. I'm going to find out just who *anonymous* is if it's the last thing I ever do."

"Well, good luck with that. I just think he's so slippery we'll never be able to get to the bottom of his crooked dealings. I'm telling you, Ned, this guy is good. He's really, really good." Elmer sat back in his chair and shook his head.

"Oh, I'm going to get to the bottom of it all. And when I do, I'm convinced that the federal authorities will want to know what I discover."

"Don't forget his wife." Judith smirked. "She needs to be brought down as well. She's just so full of herself. The women in this church are disgusted with her. She just prances all over town in her little size zero dresses. She needs to live a simpler lifestyle. You know. The kind that's more fitting for a minister's wife."

A smile crossed Ned's face. "Oh, I've not forgotten his wife. She'll get hers as well."

Judith met Ned's smile with an even bigger one of her own. She giggled in anticipation. "Oh, Ned. Tell me. Tell me."

Ned just nodded a confident look. "Let's just say that she's going to get hers. That's all you need to know for now. The both of them are going to reap all that they've been sowing."

Judith clapped her hands together. "Oh, thank you Ned. Thank you so much." Judith closed her eyes and lifted her hands in prayer. She uttered, "Thank you, Jesus, for giving us such a faithful leader in your servant Ned. Together with him, we'll be able to save our wonderful church from destruction." When she opened her eyes she looked gratefully at her husband and then at Ned, "You know what? I feel like celebrating. Let's order banana splits."

CHAPTER 40

"Father Austin, this is Stephen over at Noah's House."

Steele's stomach did a flip. He immediately feared another disaster over at the safe house. Even though things appeared to be settled and the controversy around the safe house had subsided, he was still anxious that something unforeseen would show up and start the controversy all over again. He asked nervously, "Is there anything wrong?"

Stephen chuckled. "No, don't worry. There's nothing wrong. It's just that we have a delivery over here and I don't know what to do with it."

"What kind of delivery?"

"There are two guys here with a tree. They said it's a gift for Noah's House."

"What kind of tree is it?"

"They said it's a saucer magnolia."

Steele frowned. "What the heck is a saucer magnolia?"

"Oh, Father Austin, you've seen them around town. They're the first ones to bloom in the spring. They usually bloom in late January or February. They have big pink flowers on them."

Steele started nodding. "You mean the ones with flowers that look like big pink tulips?"

"Yeah, those are the ones. They flower first and then they get their leaves."

"I can see a couple of them right now outside my office window here in the First Church Cemetery. That's a very pretty tree. I just didn't know they were a magnolia tree.

"What do you want me to do with it?"

"Who's it from?"

"The nursery guys don't know. They just said they had instructions to deliver it and to plant it in front of Noah's House."

"Is there a place to plant it out front?"

"I guess so. They've already put it out there on the front line. It's a pretty good size tree already. It's in full bloom right now. It looks good sitting out there. There's plenty of room for it."

"Well, if it's all paid for and everything, I guess that it would be acceptable."

"The men tell me that everything is paid for and we only have to give them the go ahead and they'll plant it for us."

"Gosh, I don't see any reason not to accept the gift. Tell them to go ahead, but make sure that it's not put in a spot that will cause us problems later."

"Like I said, Father, there's plenty of room on the front lawn. We were going to need to do some planting out there anyway." Then Stephen started chuckling. "Hey guys, look out there at the tree. Do you see him?"

"What's going on, Stephen? What do you see?"

"Father Austin, I wish you could see this. A red-breasted robin is sitting in that tree. He's all nestled down. It looks like he thinks he's found a new home."

"Can you get a picture of him?"

"I'll try. Why?"

"Stephen, my grandmother always told me that the person that saw the first robin in the spring would have good luck. Maybe that robin sitting in that pink magnolia is just God's way of letting us know that Noah's House is blessed and is going to have good luck from this day forward."

"I'll try to get a picture of him before the men start planting the tree. He doesn't look like he plans on moving any time soon."

"That would just be great. I'd like to have the picture to look at from time to time. Maybe it will help remind me that all the struggles are well worth the results."

"They are, Father, they are. These kids are safe here. They can be themselves in this place. We've done a good thing. We've given these teenagers a place that they can call home."

"I agree, Stephen. It's just that when the battle is on, it's so tempting to just give up."

"I know. If the picture of the robin doesn't give you some hope, then just come over here and spend some time with these kids."

"Thanks, Stephen. Thanks for your ministry. And thanks for being a friend."

"Don't mention it. Now, there is one more thing."

"What's that?"

"They have a note addressed to you. They said it came with the purchase order for the tree."

"Do you have it?"

"I've got it right here."

"Does it have a name or address or anything on it?"

"No."

"Did you ask them how the tree was paid for?"

"They said the order was paid for in cash."

"Wow, this mystery just gets deeper and deeper." Steele thought for a minute. "Tell you what, go ahead and open the note. Read it to me."

"You sure? I mean, it's addressed to you."

"It's okay. Go ahead and open it."

"Here goes. Gosh, this is kind of strange."

"Oh?"

"Yeah, I'll read it to you. *Dear Father Austin, please plant this tree in front of Noah's House. It's a gift from a friend of your ministry. My only request is that you ask Almeda to oversee its planting and care.*"

"Is that all? Is it signed?"

"No, it's not signed. That's all it says. Do you have any idea who it's from?"

Steele smiled.

EPILOGUE

Steele was sitting at his desk. He had just finished saying his morning prayers. He was thankful for so much. He was grateful for his beautiful wife and his little family. They were all happy to finally be in a home of their own. Travis was in a neighborhood play group. Amanda was beginning to focus on Steele's face when he held her. She would smile at him. He could blow on her stomach and she would laugh.

Things at the parish were going smoothly. The new member minister reported a ten percent growth in new members over the past year. The pledges and offerings were coming in above what the finance committee had projected for this time of year. He was excited about starting a new seminar on marriage. Several of the couples in the parish had asked him to teach a course on Christian Marriage and Family Life.

Noah's House was being completely renovated. Every Sunday about half the teens attended worship at First Church. A few of them still had a rather flamboyant dress code. Steele had quietly smiled to himself to see some of the more properly dressed folk point at the kids and whisper. Their whispers were often followed with disapproving looks.

Just then Steele heard something being shoved under his closed office door. It was a large brown envelope. He wasn't expecting a delivery from any messengers. He walked over to the door and retrieved the envelope. He returned to his desk, opened the envelope and removed the contents. There were three large photographs in it. He looked at the first. It was a picture of Randi. She was sitting on a lounge chair. Her swimming suit top was unsnapped. She was holding onto it while a very muscular young man appeared to be rubbing suntan lotion on her back. He quickly moved to the second picture. It too was of Randi. She was standing facing the young man. Their hips were touching. She was still clutching her unsnapped top. She had one of her hands on the young man's chest. Steele felt his legs grow weak. He collapsed into his chair. He then looked at the third picture. It was a close up of the two of them.

She was still clutching her open swimming suit top. He had his hands on her waist. Their bodies were pressed together. Their lips were just an inch apart. It was apparent that she had either just kissed the stranger or was about to kiss him. He spread the pictures out on his desk. He rubbed at his eyes. He strained to look at them. The pictures started to blur. Once again he struggled to focus, but his vision was clouded. Large tears streamed down his face and dropped onto his desk.

COMING IN THE FALL OF 2009
BOOK FIVE IN THE MAGNOLIA SERIES
"THE SWEET MAGNOLIA"

ABOUT THE AUTHOR

The Reverend Doctor Dennis R. Maynard has been a priest in the Episcopal Church for thirty-seven years. He has served parishes in Oklahoma, Texas, South Carolina, and California. The author of eight books, he is often requested to be a guest speaker or preacher in congregations and communities throughout the nation. He has also served as a consultant or retreat leader to some sixty parishes and Dioceses.

Doctor Maynard and his wife, Nancy, have parented four children. He retired from full-time parish work in 2003. He lives in Rancho Mirage, California.

All of Doctor Maynard's books can be ordered through his website at www.Episkopols.com, through Amazon.com, or any of the online bookstores. If you would like to have Doctor Maynard visit your parish or organization as a guest speaker or preacher, please visit his website or e-mail him at Episkopols@aol.com.

WWW.EPISKOPOLS.COM

BOOKS FOR CLERGY AND THE PEOPLE THEY SERVE

3561333

Made in the USA